BOOK REVIEWS

"The Honorable Cowboy's Convenient Marriage is the third title in the 7 Brides for 7 Cowboys series, yet I easily read it as a stand-alone title since I've not read the earlier titles in this series. Anything I might have needed to know was smoothly covered either in the narrative or dialogue so I didn't feel lost at all.

Both Dakota and Sarah have painful pasts, and both have dealt with similar issues, each in their own unique way. Sarah is open, loving, and, in many ways naive. She's loved Dakota for years, something she's kept to herself mostly for he'd broken her innocent heart with his declaration of never intending to commit himself to a woman for life.

Now, Dakota has his reasons for that attitude, and in his mind, they might be good ones, but he's closed himself off out of fear. Not for himself but for those he loves, a wife, perhaps children. So he won't take the risk. After an injury in the line of duty, he

left his FBI position to open his own Private Investigation company specializing in finding missing or kidnapped children. It is the case of a missing child that brings him home once again, and into danger... and possibly the love of his life if he's willing to set aside his fears."
~Marsha

"Lifelong friends Dakota and Sarah embark on a marriage of convenience that is to their mutual benefit and also on a background of trying to find a kidnapped child. Likeable characters, especially when they get out of their own way and admit their true feelings. Enjoyable read."
~AliR

THE HONORABLE COWBOY'S CONVENIENT MARRIAGE

MELODY ARCHER

WANT TO READ MORE SWEET ROMANCE?

Eliza and Daniel Stevenson's love story is waiting for you to enjoy. Get your copy of this Free Sweet and Clean Romance today!
Go here: https://memorablefictionbooks.com/pages/pb-free-book

akota

DAKOTA CALLAHAN STOOD MOTIONLESS, his gaze captured by the mountains in the distance.

His large office window in Denver, Colorado gave him a spectacular view of the tall snow capped mountains.

A longing flooded him to leave sooner than planned, for his family's ranch in Montana.

He would leave today.

Decision made, Dakota turned and his dark eyes swept across his office desk. Quickly, he made a mental note of what he needed to bring with him.

As he started gathering the papers and documents he needed for this next case, his dark eyes landing on a faded photo.

With a shaky hand, he picked it up.

His finger shook slightly as he gently traced the slightly tattered picture of a little girl's smiling face.

A tight knot formed in his belly, as it usually did when memories from his childhood swirled around and around.

Only a short time after that photo was taken, his little sister disappeared without a trace.

Regret clung to him like a scab that refused to heal. He had failed to keep his little sister safe on that day years ago.

Anger flooded him as he remembered. It was that same anger that later propelled him into law enforcement, and eventually into his career as an FBI agent.

He had become skilled at looking for missing persons and because of that, he'd searched and found many kidnappers.

Searching for missing children was still his passion today.

Quickly, he slipped the photo into his briefcase. He placed it next to the picture of Mindy, the little girl that was his focus for this next case.

From what he knew of Mindy's parents and the few clues he'd uncovered, he had a hunch that the trail would lead him near his hometown in the Montana mountains.

Chase and Amanda Ballenger were friends of his. They had recently moved away from Montana to live in Colorado, because of Chase's new job.

The fear he saw in Amanda's eyes when he went to their house to ask them questions about the day Mindy disappeared, made him more determined than ever to find their daughter.

He was eager to solve this case. Nothing would give

him greater pleasure than putting another kidnapper behind bars and bringing another innocent little girl back to the arms of her loving family.

His German Shepherd barked loudly, interrupting his thoughts. His dog sat on his haunches in the middle of the room, his tail swishing back and forth in his eagerness to get going.

Turning, Dakota spoke in low tones. "Settle down, Sarge."

Immediately, his dog lay down on the rug with a loud moan.

Dakota grinned and shook his head.

His dog was an excellent tracker and a well-disciplined dog most of the time, except on days like today when he was feeling impatient.

He sighed. It looked like he had everything that was needed for this trip. Reaching down, he double-checked the straps that held his handgun in place.

As a Private Investigator who was dealing with catching serious offenders, Dakota had received his license to carry a concealed weapon. All his years of training at the police academy and with the FBI, had prepared him on how to handle serious offenders.

He only hoped it wouldn't come to that as he worked to solve this case.

Closing his laptop case, he turned and grabbed his cowboy hat. With one last look around his office, he opened his office door.

With a short whistle, his dog stood to his feet, hurrying after him. His German Shepherd was always happiest when he was active. Which made Sarge the best dog he could ask for. When chasing the bad guys, Dakota was particularly grateful to have his faithful watchdog by his side.

Stopping for a moment, he spoke to his secretary. "I'll be out of the office for two weeks. But if you find any useful leads in your research on the Ballenger case, be sure to call me."

"I will, Mr. Callahan." Cameron Ortez nodded quickly as she shuffled the large stack of papers in her hands. He had hired the thirty-five-year-old single mom two years ago, right after he found her missing daughter.

Dakota had searched for two weeks, before he finally found her seven-year-old daughter living with Cameron's ex-husband and his girlfriend in a deserted farmhouse. His dog had followed a scent and had also uncovered a stash of drugs.

Needless to say, the little girl was brought home safe and sound to her mother.

Ever since that day, his secretary had been very loyal and a big help in every one of the missing children's cases he took on.

"You can count on me. After all you've done for me, it's little enough to do in return." Cameron blinked back the tell-tale sign of moisture in her brown eyes.

Dakota smiled. "We agreed. There'll be no more talk of paying me back or anything like that. I was glad to help. And now, we work together to bring down the bad guys, right?"

"Yeah, we do. Thanks boss." She nodded, a pleased smile lighting up her face.

"Okay then. Thanks for taking care of things here. Talk

to you later." Dakota smiled and put his black cowboy hat on his dark hair. He stepped outside into the brisk fall air, hurrying towards his truck.

His dog trotted happily behind him.

As he opened the truck door, Sarge jumped onto the bench seat, finding a comfortable spot to sit on his haunches.

Suddenly, the loud ringing from his phone filled the air. Reaching down to the leather case attached to his belt, he pulled out his phone.

"Callahan, here."

"Hey, Dakota. Thought I'd call and check in. How's the shoulder?" Tony Marletti was a good friend and his former partner at the FBI.

"Still aches, but it's on the mend." Dakota rotated his shoulder in a circular motion. The dull ache was a reminder of the gunshot wound he'd received from a suspect they'd been following.

The wound had needed immediate surgery to repair the motor function of his shoulder and left arm. It was because of the seriousness of the wound, that the FBI told him they'd been left with no alternative but to recommend early retirement.

"I'm glad to hear it. And I must say, I miss you, man. You were the best partner I've ever had."

"Thanks, Tony. That means a lot to hear you say that. It was the same for me. I miss having a partner like you to solve these kidnapping cases I've taken on."

"How's it going in your new duties as a PI?"

Dakota leaned against the side of the truck, one hand rubbing the stubble on his chin. "There are pros and cons.

I definitely have more freedom as a Private Investigator than I ever did as an FBI agent."

"However, it's only me and a new PI that I hired part-time, to work on these cases. Tracking down people is a big job, and it forces me to be on high alert much of the time."

"Yeah, that's rough. But I have faith in you. You'll find the suspect. You always were the best tracker in the FBI."

"Well, I'm counting on finding this one. I'm headed back to my home town in Montana. The clues are leading me there. I'll visit the family ranch for a few days as well. Maybe that will help me get a fresh perspective."

"Good. Going home always served you well in the past."

Dakota smiled. "Yeah it has. But enough about me. How's it going for you?"

"Keeping busy as usual. But I do have some exciting news."

"What's that?"

"I'm soon to be a married man." There was an eagerness in his friend's voice that he'd never heard before.

"So, you finally asked Olivia to marry you?" Dakota grinned. "I'm happy for the two of you."

Tony chuckled. "It took me quite a while to get her to agree to marry me, but I finally did it."

Dakota remembered when his friend had first started dating Olivia three years ago. At the start Olivia hadn't been too sure of Tony and it took her a while before she began to trust him. It seemed his friend had finally won over the woman he loved.

"That's great, Tony. You sound happy."

"I am."

Dakota could tell from his friend's satisfied chuckle that statement was true. In that moment, a pang of longing hit him hard.

What would it be like to have a wife by his side?

There had only been one woman in the past that he had loved. But, because of what happened between them, she had run away from him. He didn't really know the reason for her fear, but he figured it was because of something he'd said or done.

It didn't change the fact that it was much too late for any sort of relationship to grow between the two of them.

Tony interrupted his thoughts. "What about you Dakota? Are you dating someone?"

"No." Dakota responded quickly. He didn't really want to dive into the details. "I'm far too busy to date."

Tony chuckled on the other end of the phone line. Dakota tightened his jawline in irritation at his friend.

"Dakota, I recall you speaking very fondly about a woman from your small town. Maybe it's time to win back the one woman who captured your heart years ago."

Dakota sighed. He remembered Tony was like a dog with a bone when he smelled the scent of an unsolved mystery.

He might as well get it over with.

"I don't think that's possible. At least not anymore."

"Why not?"

Dakota sighed. "I think I ruined any chance I had when I saw her a couple of years ago. It was around the time of my father's funeral and I was out of my mind with grief."

He grimaced as memories came back of that day a

couple of years ago. Sarah had been at his dad's funeral. Later that day, she'd found him up the mountain by the waterfall, where he often went to think.

They had spent more time together during the week that Dakota had been home. He cared for Sarah, but in spite of that, he couldn't make any sort of commitment.

Fear stopped him from doing so.

No, he wasn't going to put any woman he loved in a position where she was worried every day for his safety. And most importantly, he wasn't going to risk the life of his wife if one of the suspects decided to come after his family to try to harm them.

That was the biggest reason he backed away from commitment, and especially, marriage.

Regret weighed heavy in Dakota's heart because he was convinced he'd hurt Sarah with his refusal to offer her more.

"Perhaps you'll get a second chance."

"No, I'm afraid that's not likely." The stinging pain of regret pierced his heart.

Tony sighed. "You've never been a man who gives up on something he wants, Dakota. Don't give up now."

Dakota grunted as he mulled over his friend's words. He shoved his laptop case onto the front seat of his truck. "While I appreciate the encouragement, it won't change anything. I'm glad we could talk, Tony. It was good to catch up. But, I've got to run."

Tony chuckled. "Alright then. Enjoy yourself. And Callahan? I hope you don't let any kind of fear stop you from taking a chance on love, my friend. I can tell you, love is the best thing that's happened to me."

"I'll keep your fair words in mind, Tony. Talk to you later." Dakota ended the call on his smartphone and slid onto the front seat of his truck.

As he drove the long stretch of highway from Colorado towards his family's Montana home, his thoughts returned to Tony's words.

Don't let fear stop you from taking a chance on love, my friend.

A picture of Sarah popped unbidden into his mind. He could still see her in his mind's eye the last time she stood on the mountain. Her strawberry blonde hair blowing in the wind, her green eyes wide and filled with trust.

It was trust he didn't deserve.

Guilt and regret had been his constant companions ever since that day two years ago.

Now that he was going home for a few days, he would need to make a point of talking with Sarah again. He needed to fix things between them.

But first he would touch base with his mom and brothers. It had been a long while since he'd seen them last.

Dakota made a mental note to connect with Milo Stevens, the part-time Private Investigator who worked for him. While Milo was working to finish the Waters case, Dakota would be doing what he could to find Mindy Barrenger. The parents were counting on him and so was the missing little girl.

Dakota sighed as he slowed his truck and turned up the long road that led to the Triple C ranch.

Home.

He parked his truck near the sprawling ranch house.

As he got out of the truck, he was greeted enthusiastically by Jack and Jill, the Callahan family's faithful Bernese Mountain dogs.

His dog jumped down, positioning his furry body in a protective stance.

"Settle down, Sarge." The dog sat on his haunches obeying Dakota's command.

It had been so long since he'd been back to the ranch, that even his faithful dog seemed to forget this place.

Dakota loved having the protection of his furry companion, but some days he needed to step in and force his dog to stand down.

He patted Sarge's head for obeying so quickly and walked toward the ranch house.

Hurrying up the steps, he opened the door, happy to see his mom hurrying towards him with arms open wide.

"Son, you've come home. I'm so happy to see you." Annie Callahan slipped her slender arms around him, pulling him into a hug.

He kissed the top of her head and embraced his mom. Warmth and a sense of belonging flooded him. It was good to be home again.

"You look tired, Dakota." His mother stepped back and placed a wrinkled gentle hand on either side of his face, looking deeply into his eyes. "You've been working too hard."

She'd always had an uncanny ability to see right through him. "There have been a few late nights, but I'm okay. Besides I'm home for a few more days now. That has its own way of energizing me."

She eyed him for a moment, before nodding. "I'm glad. You look like you need it."

Dakota smiled and nodded. "It's always a pleasure to visit you, mom."

A happy smile turned his mother's lips upwards and her eyes brightened at his words.

Without warning, the connecting door from the porch to the kitchen burst open and one by one his six brothers made their way onto the large porch.

He was soon surrounded by embraces from his brothers. Dakota was also given a big hug by Wyatt's wife Abby and Denver's wife Sierra. Abby held her three-month old daughter in her arms. The baby was the spitting image of her mother with her auburn hair and large green eyes.

An unexpected surge of longing for a family of his own hit his belly as he watched them. It irritated him, that he would have any kind of yearning for a family of his own.

He experienced a similar burst of longing when he hugged Denver and his wife Sierra who was seven months pregnant. Already, Dakota was anxious for their family supper to be over so he could do something else — anything — to escape all these uncomfortable feelings.

They all followed their mother to the dining room.

Dakota tousled the heads of his three nephews, Tony, Joey and Cody as they walked towards the dining room.

The boys bombarded him with questions.

"How long are you staying, Uncle Dakota?" Tony persisted.

"I'm not sure on that. A couple of weeks, maybe longer." Dakota was careful not to give a firm answer, knowing how quickly things could change given what he did for a living.

"Aww, I was hoping for longer. Can all of us do something fun together?"

The hopeful look in all three boys' faces, nearly was his undoing. He couldn't disappoint them. "Well, maybe we can think of something to do together. I'm not sure what day will work, but let's plan on it, okay?"

"Thanks Uncle Dakota. You're the best." Tony's happy smile was echoed by his two other nephews.

"You're welcome." Dakota grinned as the boys went to sit by their parents.

His mother smiled and waved at him, patting the chair next to her, indicating that he should sit by her side. Happily, he obeyed her instructions.

As soon as they were all seated around the familiar large wooden table, Annie Callahan smiled lovingly to each of her sons and their families before she spoke.

"I'm so glad each of us could be together today." Her blue eyes glistened with unshed tears.

Dakota shifted uncomfortably as a surge of raw emotions stirred in his belly.

"I wish your father could be here to see each of you now. He would often tell me, how he couldn't wait to see our sons' lovely wives and their children. It means so much to me, to have you all here today." His mother's gaze swept the table, a warm smile on her face.

"Maybe, Grandpa is watching all of us from Heaven, Grandma." Cody's replied.

To Dakota's way of thinking, Cody's words seemed to hold the wisdom of the ages.

"I'm sure that's true, darling. Thank you for reminding me Cody." There was a shine in Annie Callahan's eyes as her gaze rested on her grandson. "Well, in that case maybe each of us should share one thing we love about being a part of the Callahan family."

"Can I go first, Grandma?" Cody was eager to share.

"Of course, Cody."

The seven year old looked around the table at his uncles, aunts and cousins. With a smile he spoke with confidence. "I love being a Callahan because this family loves you no matter how many mistakes you make or how you might look. It's the same reason I love my animals. They love me no matter what… just like the Callahan family does."

"Well said, son." Denver squeezed his shoulder, looking at Cody with a father's pride that brought back memories for Dakota. Cody had been welcomed into the family when he was six years old, after the family learned that he was Denver's son.

It warmed his heart to hear his nephew speak of the acceptance and love he felt from the Callahan family.

That feeling was similar to how his father — Mack Callahan — made him feel when he was first adopted into this large ranching family.

After Cody spoke up, everyone else took turns around the table, talking about what they loved most about the Callahan family.

However, Dakota continued to replay his youngest nephew's words in his mind.

As a young boy, he remembered feeling that he was loved no matter how he looked and no matter how many mistakes he made. Which was quite a change from how he had been treated as a young boy in school.

Coming into the Callahan family, had given him a lot of gifts for which to be grateful.

It seemed Cody had the intuitive awareness that all children did of knowing when they were loved.

As he looked around a warmth swept through him, knowing that same sense of acceptance he felt as a young boy was still here today.

He enjoyed being back at the ranch jawing with his brothers, and the evening meal passed by quickly.

They were just finishing dessert, when Hunter asked him. "Are you sticking around for a while?"

"Yeah, for a week or two. Hoping to get some perspective and some real leads on a new case I'm working on."

Hunter nodded. "You should go up the mountain to visit some of your old trails. You used to tell me it was where you found real peace and clarity."

Dakota nodded. "I think you're right. Maybe I'll do that tomorrow."

❧

BY THE TIME he'd walked the steep incline towards the heart of the mountain, Dakota was breathing heavily. His warm breath created swirls that mingled in the cool mountain air.

Breathing in the cool air refreshed him, body and soul.

He had skirted around Angus MacDonald's farm, about a mile back. Seeing Sarah again — or her grandfather — was something he wasn't ready to do just yet.

With that decision made, Dakota walked further north.

He missed having his dog by his side today.

His furry companion was spending time with his nephews today. They had asked him repeatedly, until he finally gave in. He'd take his dog with him next time.

Besides, today he was simply walking to clear his head and to gain a new perspective on the case he was working on.

He only had a couple of clues that led to Refuge Mountain, but he'd always followed his gut. And this time it was telling him that somewhere in this small town was the kidnapper and Mindy.

As Dakota's thoughts swirled with questions. He was so focused on trying to uncover the answers, that he suddenly found that he had walked so far and arrived at an unfamiliar area of the mountain. Looking around, it seemed like a secluded area.

Thick rows of pine trees surrounded him as did the mountains. He stood near an embankment that led down to a small creek. The faint sound of trickling water amid the quietness of the mountain, was soothing and just what he needed.

Peering farther north, he spotted a swirling cloud of smoke rising from a small cabin in the distance.

Suddenly, a loud crack of thunder split the sky overhead, and a light rain began to fall.

Pulling the hood of his jacket over his head, he looked at the cabin again.

Curious, he began walking toward it.

Dakota had only gone a short distance, when without warning, a deafening and sharp boom filled the air.

A sudden pain seared his left leg and he fell to the ground.

In shock, he looked down at his leg only to see blood already pooling on his thigh. Reaching for the hand-held gun at his side, he pulled it out to defend himself. As he looked around he couldn't see anyone.

Someone shot him. Why would they do that?

Struggling with questions, he took off the belt from around his waist and made a makeshift tourniquet to slow the flow of blood.

Reaching inside his jacket pocket, he pulled out his two-way radio. Dakota was thankful for this long-range radio that could reach someone in the family within a five-mile range.

In his estimation, he was only about three miles from the ranch, so connecting with someone in the family should be simple.

With shaky hands he called the ranch house. No one answered. He tried calling a few times, with no answer.

Now what was he going to do? He tried to stand on his good leg, but the pain was so unbearable that he fell down to the ground, welcoming the blackness.

Sarah MacDonald had just turned her bay horse around to head back home, when suddenly the booming sound of a gunshot caused her to stop.

Looking around, she tried to see if there was a poacher nearby. She couldn't see through the pouring rain. There were only two other times she could recall, when there had been a poacher near her Grandfather's land.

Curious as to what was going on, Sarah turned her mare around and headed North. The rain pelted her face, and she pulled the hood of her rain jacket over her head.

Urging her horse to go faster, Sarah kept going until she spotted the smoke swirling toward the sky from a small cabin in the distance. She had roamed these mountains ever since she was a little girl and knew them well.

Normally she made it a rule not to get too close to a stranger's property. When she didn't see anyone in the vicinity, she turned back.

She was about to urge her horse faster, when she spotted a jacket behind a tree.

Drawing up closer, she saw that it was a man lying motionless on the ground.

Quickly, she jumped off her horse, letting the reins hang to the ground. Her well-trained mare would keep still until she returned.

Nearing the body, she gasped when she caught sight of the patch of blood covering his leg.

His body lay in an awkward position, his one hand holding what looked like a hand-held radio.

Her heart thundered in fear. Someone had shot this man. Who would commit such a horrible deed? What happened?

With one hand, she pushed back the black cowboy hat that lay half-way across his face and inhaled a quick breath.

Dakota Callahan.

The same man who had caused her so much pain and heartache had returned.

Whatever the reason, all she knew was that he desperately needed her help now.

Hurriedly, Sarah bent down to help him.

She would see to it that he got the help he needed. But anything beyond basic care, she wasn't going volunteer.

Sarah had already decided years ago when Dakota caused her pain, that she would never surrender her heart to this man again.

arah

Dr. Weston slipped the medical supplies inside his black bag, looking at his patient one last time.

Sarah followed the doctor's gaze to see Dakota lying motionless on the bed, sound asleep.

She was grateful that the doctor had arrived as quickly as he did. From the moment she found Dakota on the mountain with deep wounds, she had worried about him.

Sarah and her grandfather managed to help him into their cabin. Through a lot of effort, she was able to boost Dakota up onto her horse's back to bring him back to her grandfather's home.

Dakota insisted that they call the retired doctor that lived nearby. He refused to go to the hospital. Then he had told them not to worry because he would explain everything to Sheriff Turnbull.

Reluctantly, Sarah and her grandfather said they would agree to his terms — if Doctor Weston assured them his wound would heal well enough without a trip to the hospital.

Sarah was fearful the leg wound might get worse, but she also knew how stubborn Dakota could be.

She was eager for the doctor to arrive and look at his leg wound.

Her grandfather called the doctor who arrived quickly, much to Sarah's relief.

While the doctor was talking with grandfather, Sarah had taken a moment to call Dakota's brother Hunter, so his family would know what happened and where he was.

Sarah was glad she remembered to call. In all of the panic over Dakota's bleeding leg, she forgot about how concerned his family would be about him.

Looking at the doctor, Sarah breathed a sigh of relief. It was reassuring to know that Dakota would be in the doctor's capable hands.

Doctor Weston had done his fair share of digging out unwanted bullets and other surgeries at their local Hospital in Refuge Mountain.

Although he opted for an early retirement a few years ago, he continued to help people in the farms and ranches that surrounded their small town.

In fact, the doctor had stopped by last year, when her Grandfather had developed a bad infection in his chest.

Sarah was grateful that he was available.

After he had finished examining Dakota, they followed the doctor towards the front door.

"It was a serious wound. However, the good news is that the bullet appears to have only hit the soft tissue in his leg and missed hitting the bone. He needs to stay here to rest and heal. But, if he continues to improve, the wound should be healed in two weeks."

She sighed in relief. "Good. Were you able to clean the wound?"

"Yes. There were only small bits of debris that needed to be cleaned, and now the wound should heal well enough. I gave him a sedative and a little something to help ease the pain." The doctor slipped on his coat.

"Is there something I can do to help?" Sarah wanted to do what she could to get Dakota back on his feet. The sooner the better. The man who had been like her best friend since childhood, was now too close for her comfort.

"Yes, there is." Doctor Weston nodded and opened his medical bag. "You can clean the wounded area and put on clean bandages on his leg twice a day, that is what is needed right now."

The doctor handed her a pack of clean gauze and an antiseptic cream. "Watchful care for our patient for the next few days is very important."

"Of course. I'll take care of it." She assured Dr. Weston.

Even though it was difficult to be in close proximity to the man she still had tender feelings for, Sarah was determined to do her duty.

The doctor nodded quickly. "Good. Well, I need to be going."

"Do you want some tea before you go?"

"Thanks for the offer Sarah, but I'll need to take a rain check. I have a woman on these mountains who is ready to deliver her fifth child. I better not take up any more time, or the baby will arrive before I do."

Dr. Weston smiled warmly and reached for his hat. "But I will be back tomorrow to check on that wound. Call me if his fever gets worse."

"I will." Sarah replied. After watching the doctor drive away, she closed the door.

Her dog limped towards the door, barking at the sound of the car as the doctor drove away.

"Shh, Maisie." With a gentle hand, Sarah patted her Coonhound's head, settling her down. Immediately, Maisie moved her brown body closer to Sarah and stopped barking.

Maisie's body trembled somewhat, a sure sign that she was still uncomfortable around vehicles. She had been wounded when Sarah first found her lying in a ditch two years ago.

Sarah brought the dog to the Veterinarian who put a splint on the fractured leg. It took three months before the leg was healed, but to this day Maisie didn't like the sound of vehicles.

In spite of searching for the dog's owner for weeks, no one ever claimed her. That's when her grandfather said, Sarah might as well keep the dog as it seemed Maisie was already attached to her.

Sarah was all too happy to agree.

Putting away the memory, Sarah walked toward her grandfather, with Maisie limping along behind her.

"It looks like Doctor Weston is on his way to help deliver Sorcha Maguire's fifth baby. I hope all goes well for her and the little one."

"Aye. Your grandmother loved to see all the children born in this area. She would have given her right arm, to have more children of her own. But, she was only able to give birth to one baby — your father. The doctor warned her that having any more would be the death of her."

Sarah walked over to the wooden mantle that sat over the fireplace and picked up the photo of her grandmother and grandfather on their wedding day.

The old photo, taken on their wedding over fifty years ago, had always been a reminder to her that sometimes love lasts. Her grandmother had passed away from cancer when she was sixteen. The pain of loss still lingered for both of them.

She set the picture down, peering over at her grandfather.

The gray haired man she loved so much, walked over to his easy chair and sat down, looking out the window as the evening sky darkened.

A deep furrow formed between his brows.

"Do you want me to make some tea?" Sarah knew he was missing the love of his life. Maybe sharing a hot cup of tea together would help.

On most evenings, they sat together. The comfort they brought to each other, helped to soothe their woes.

"That would be just the thing, Sarah."

Sarah put the kettle on the stove to boil and reached into the cupboard to grab their two favorite mugs.

She loved it when they shared a little conversation and tea in the evening.

"I'm just going to check on Dakota and I'll be right back." Sarah walked over to her bedroom and peered inside.

It looked like Dakota had fallen asleep. She left the door open a crack in case he awoke.

As she returned to the kitchen and poured the tea, Sarah hoped their patient would rest well so he could heal.

The scent of alfalfa tea wafted upwards as she carried it to the sitting room.

"This tea should help relieve some of the pain and swelling in your joints, grandfather." Sarah set his tea down on the side table near his chair.

She noticed the somber expression on her grandfather's face.

"You're worrying about something, or planning something. Which is it?" Sarah took a small sip from her hot drink, peering over at her grandfather.

Angus MacDonald chuckled softly, shaking his head. "I forget how well you know me."

Sarah smiled and waited. If she were patient, he would soon talk about what was bothering him.

"I was thinking again on how I long to see you settled, granddaughter. It would bring such joy to your dear old grandfather's heart."

Sarah sighed, a small smile playing around her lips. "When you say you want me settled, what you really mean is you want to see me married."

"Aye. I do."

"I know you want what's best for me grandfather, but I'm not ready to marry. I'm just fine living here with you and helping to take care of you." Sarah protested.

Her grandfather's gaze lingered on her as one hand rubbed his gray whiskers. "I'm fine. You don't need to stay here to care for me."

"Grandfather, do you remember last winter when you caught that bad chest cold?"

At his nod, she continued. "At the time, you were grateful both Doctor Weston and I were nearby to help you. But, I worry about you living here on the mountain. I think maybe you should move to town."

Angus grimaced. "I know you worry dear Sarah." He shook his head, his jaw set in determination. "But, I don't want to move to town. My life is here on this mountain — in the same place I lived with your grandmother. That won't ever change."

Sarah knew her grandfather had what her grandmother used to describe as the Scottish stubbornness in him. Once he'd set his mind on something, he hardly ever budged.

She worried for him and feared the day would come when he would be forced to move away.

"Well, we don't need to think about that now. We need to help our guest to get well first."

"Aye, that's true." Her grandfather smothered a yawn.

"Grandfather, you should get your rest. I'll keep watch over Dakota tonight, in case he wakes."

Her grandfather stood to his feet and began to walk towards his bedroom. "That's kind of you, Sarah. I am tired. If you need a break, come wake me and I'll keep an eye on our patient."

Sarah smiled. "Thanks." She stood to her feet and reached her arms around him in a big hug. "I love you, grandfather."

For a moment she was wrapped in his strong arms and held tightly to his chest. He kissed her cheek gently. "I love you too, granddaughter."

Sarah watched as he limped towards his bedroom. His arthritis seemed to be bothering him more tonight. He had been on his feet a lot more today, which was likely the cause of increased aches and pains.

He needed his rest.

She hoped he would feel better by morning.

Sarah bit her lip. Worry gnawed at her. This past year, she noticed her grandfather had become increasingly tired and not as steady on his feet as he once was.

She needed her grandfather, especially on days like this when the unexpected happened. But she also realized that he wouldn't be by her side forever.

Sighing, she stood to her feet.

Changes were coming everywhere she looked lately. She rubbed the knot that formed in her belly, hoping it would go away soon.

It seemed life was spinning out of control. Ever since she was a little girl, big changes made her fearful and vulnerable.

With shaky hands, she fingered the mustard seed necklace that she always wore. Her grandmother had given her the necklace when Sarah had first came to live with them.

At the end of a gold chain, lay a tiny mustard seed tucked away inside a tiny glass box.

The memory of her grandmother's words as she placed the necklace around her neck, had stayed with her to this day.

Faith the size of this mustard seed is all the faith you need to move the mountains in your life. You've needed faith to help with the loss of your dad and mom, who died far too soon and later with all the hurt from your stepfather.

Remember, your birth parents loved you with all their hearts. Treasure that love, believe in yourself and have faith always. Having faith as small as this mustard seed, will give you the strength to face any difficulties that come your way.

Swallowing back emotion, she nodded as her fingers let go of the locket.

One other thing her grandmother had said, that Sarah never forgot. *I'm asking you to forgive your stepfather. Not because he needs it, but because you need to forgive him. Do this, so a root of bitterness doesn't grow inside of you and swallow up all the happiness in your life.*

Sarah promised her grandmother that she would do as she asked. But, there was a big part of her that hoped she would never see her stepfather again.

But, if that day ever came, she knew what she needed to do. There was no doubt in her mind, that forgiving him would be the hardest thing she'd ever done.

Pondering all of this, she walked into the room where Dakota lay sleeping.

This night and the following week, would be some of the longest days and nights she would be forced to endure.

All because she would need to be in the same room with the man she loved.

She sighed and pulled up the sofa chair next to the bed.

He was close. In fact, he was too close, but it was necessary.

She would need to hear him in case he woke up in the middle of the night and needed her help.

After she was assured that he was sleeping peacefully, Sarah settled back into the soft cushions with the throw blanket pulled around her body.

CHAPTER THREE

arah

SARAH STIRRED at the touch of a warm hand on the back of her head.

Slowly she moved, groaning at the kinks in her neck from sleeping awkwardly in the chair nearest Dakota's bed.

Lifting up her head, she noticed he was staring at her with a glint of humor dancing in his dark eyes.

"Good morning to you again, lovely Sarah." His teasing was something she had gotten used to this past week.

It had been five days since Doctor Weston had first come to examine Dakota's leg wound. Each day he had continued to heal.

Sarah was happy he was getting better, but it seemed

that one of the consequences of feeling better was that her patient was restless and easily irritated.

She rubbed the back of her neck with one hand, trying to get the kinks out of her muscles.

"Good morning." Heat crept up her neck, flooding her cheeks as she realized she had slept so near Dakota. "Sorry. I'm afraid I must have accidentally fallen asleep here last night."

She remembered waking up a couple times in the middle of the night, because Dakota was thirsty, but then she must have dozed off again.

"I'm not sorry at all. What more could I ask for than to have my own beautiful nurse looking out for me?" Dakota thought she was beautiful? But no, of course he was teasing her. That was exactly how she remembered this man from just a few short years ago.

Memories flooded her thoughts about what happened between them only a few short years ago.

She had just returned from the weekly quilting bee at A Goode Yarn. Annie Callahan had joined her and other ladies in town to finish their wedding quilt for the newest couple that was getting married.

Just after Sarah walked Annie to the large rambling house on the Callahan ranch, she spotted Dakota outside one of the empty cabins.

He was stacking wood inside the wood lean-to beside the cabin.

Dakota's mom had told her he was back home for a while, recovering from a wound he'd received in the line of duty.

Sarah hurried across the yard, happy to see him again. After all, Dakota had been her best friend ever since her grandfather had brought her home from the hospital to live in his cabin on the mountain.

Over the years, he had helped her out of many scrapes and had often come to visit her grandfather and grandmother. Dakota had even taken time out of his busy schedule to come to her grandmother's funeral. That had meant the world to her.

Now that he was wounded, she wanted to be there to help him.

"Hey Dakota. Your mom said you were back home recovering from a wound. Are you doing okay?" Sarah walked up to him.

Dakota gripped the stack of wood tighter. After setting it on the pile, he turned to her.

"I'll be fine. You don't need to worry about me, Sarah." She bit her lip at the impatience in his voice.

"But, I just want to help."

Dakota finished stacking the last of the wood and wiped the sweat off his brow. "Sarah, there's nothing you can do to help."

"Can you at least tell me what happened?"

Dakota sighed heavily. "I got shot chasing a kidnapper a few weeks back. I had surgery, but since I lost some mobility in my shoulder, my boss at the FBI told me he was forced to give me early retirement. So now I have a wounded shoulder and I've also lost my career at the FBI that I really loved. So now you know."

"I'm sorry." Sarah searched for what she could say or do to help. "Maybe you need to do something that will take your mind off of things. Want to ride the horses to the waterfall?"

"I don't know..."

"Please, Dakota? It would be fun."

Dakota smiled and sighed. "Alright."

She was happy they would spend time together. They each rode their favorite horse up the mountain and to the waterfall. They continued to do things together over the next couple weeks while Dakota was home.

The day before he was to leave, they rode one last time to the waterfall.

Together they walked close enough to hear the sound of the water.

"I love the sound of water. It's so peaceful."

"Yeah."

Dakota was frustrated, and she hoped to help calm him.

"Talk to me. You used to tell me all sorts of details, but you hardly talk to me anymore." Sarah turned to him.

She chewed on her lower lip and stole a look at him.

He shot her a penetrating look, his mouth set in annoyance.

Dakota stepped closer, watching her intently. "Yes I did. But, now you've grown up."

"Of course I've grown up. But that doesn't change anything." Sarah grew annoyed with him.

"It does to me. It means we shouldn't spend so much time together alone anymore."

"Why?" Sarah asked, puzzled.

Exasperated he sighed. "Because in the last couple of weeks we've talked and gotten closer, but I'm starting to want a lot more."

Sarah looked at him, trying to understand him.

Dakota placed his hands around her waist. "This, Sarah. I need to hold you close. To kiss you."

She released a small gasp, just before he crushed her to him, smothering her lips with his.

His kiss shocked her in its intensity, bringing her untried senses to life.

But just as quickly as he'd kissed her, he jerked away. Running his hand through his hair, Dakota's dark eyes looked tortured as though he was torn with conflicting emotions.

"I'm sorry, Sarah. I shouldn't have done that. But now you know, why we can't spend time alone anymore." Dakota's voice sounded gruff and final.

The kiss had left Sarah weak and confused. She was trying to understand him. She was puzzled by his abrupt change in mood. Her lips still tingled from his passionate kiss.

"Come on. I'll take you back to the ranch."

Still confused, Sarah rode the horse beside his back to the ranch.

After they finished brushing down the horses and putting them to pasture, Dakota turned to her. "I'm leaving tomorrow. I've decided to set up my own Private Investigation Company in Colorado. I'll be busy and I might not return for a really long time." He hesitated and spoke hurriedly. "So this is goodbye. Have a good life, Sarah."

She'd barely managed to say goodbye, before he turned and hurried away.

Sarah understood what he meant by his last words to her. She was to move on with her life and forget about him. But she didn't know how she'd be able to do that, when she loved him.

Bewildered and with her heart aching in pain, she drove back to her grandfather's cabin, wondering what happened between them.

She'd been hurt by Dakota, and knew things would never be the same between them again.

Now two years later, she still couldn't trust his teasing or his words.

But even through all the hurt and confusion she still felt from him, Sarah hadn't lost her compassion for someone who was wounded. From what she remembered about Dakota from years ago, he wouldn't want anyone feeling sorry for him.

She looked at him doubtfully, and all of sudden saw his jaw clench and his lips tightened in pain.

Compassion, increased inside Sarah as she became aware of his discomfort. From what she remembered about Dakota from years ago, he wouldn't want anyone feeling sorry for him.

Dakota had always been strong and stoic. Most likely that's what made him great at his former job as an FBI agent and now as a Private Investigator.

Doing her best to keep things lighthearted, she said. "Well, you should be grateful I'm so dedicated to seeing you get better." She reached for the pitcher of water beside his bed and poured water into a glass.

"Dr. Weston left these pain killers for you. I think you should take one this morning." She gave him the tablet. At the touch of his hand on hers, warm tingles spread up her arm.

Quickly pulling her hand from his, she plumped his pillow. It frustrated Sarah that she was so bothered by his closeness. Memories suddenly surfaced of a time when she had been much closer to this man only a few short years ago.

Mentally Sarah shook the memories loose. Instead, she forced herself to focus on the task at hand, choosing instead to keep the barrier solidly in place around her heart.

She helped him sit up and with a slightly shaky hand, gave him a glass of water.

He swallowed quickly, before once again, his dark eyes held hers. "I could get used to all this attention."

"It's better if you don't." She swallowed her frustration and grabbed the empty glass from his hand, placing it on the nightstand near the bed.

"Why not? You're not planning on deserting me so soon are you?"

She forced a smile, even though irritation with him was ever near the surface. "No. But, I believe it won't take you long before your leg is completely healed. So you see, you won't need me. You'll be gone again soon, ready to solve your next case."

"Why do I have the distinct feeling that you're eager to see me go?"

Flustered at the way his dark eyes probed hers, she turned and began cleaning up the nightstand from discarded tissues.

Sarah busied herself with cleaning. Something she had always done when she was frustrated about something.

She really didn't want to continue this conversation. At the moment, she felt backed into a corner. Talking with Dakota today, was beginning to feel far too familiar. Only a few short years ago — after she helped care for him when he was healing from the surgery on his arm — they had started talking and had begun to get close to each other.

But, all to soon their closeness was brought to an abrupt halt by Dakota himself.

He placed thick walls between them last time and she couldn't trust that he wouldn't do it again.

Dakota reached out and gently wrapped his large hand around her wrist. "Sarah, talk to me. Tell me what's going on in that beautiful head of yours."

She stopped what she was doing and slowly turned to him. His dark eyes held hers in what seemed like a timeless moment.

Warmth filled her belly and soared up to her throat. She swallowed at the warmth of his fingers against her wrist and the tender concern reflected in his brown eyes.

Sarah wanted to tell him all that was in her heart, but at the moment didn't feel she could. Doubt and uncertainty about this man had frayed the edges of the fabric of trust that had been stitched together since their childhood years together.

Perhaps it was because of the hurt that still lingered beneath the surface from their last encounter.

She pulled her wrist out of his grasp and picked up the empty glass beside the nightstand. "You don't need to worry about me, Dakota. Besides you have more important things to think about — like getting well."

At that moment, Sarah heard her grandfather welcoming someone inside their cabin.

"I need to go. Grandfather needs me." Sarah spoke quickly, hoping to leave the room in a hurry.

His jawline tightened, evidence of his frustration. "Sarah, we will talk. Sooner, rather than later, we need to talk this out between us, all right?"

"Maybe." Sarah still wasn't convinced. "First we need to get you better."

He shook his head, shifted his body and winced in pain at the sudden movement.

"See what I mean? Now relax. I'll make you some of that alfalfa tea I make grandfather. It will help to reduce any inflammation or swelling."

Dakota shook his head and sighed. "You made that for me before and I remember not liking the taste of it."

"Well, there are times when we have to take the medicine we are given — whether we like it or not." Sarah nodded quickly and ignoring the brooding look he gave her, she hurried to leave the room.

Just as Sarah was leaving, Hunter Callahan arrived. He had come to check on Dakota not long after he'd been wounded, but now he was here again.

"Brother, it looks like you're resisting the pampering from this lovely lady." At Hunter's deep voice, they both turned to see him leaning his shoulder against the door frame. His black cowboy hat hung low over his forehead as usual.

He nodded at her. "Sarah, you are looking well. It's good to see you."

Sarah looked at Dakota's brother and smiled. He'd always been nice to her. "You too, Hunter."

Hunter knew what it felt like not to belong. People still stared at him because of the physical disfigurement on his face.

A deep scar ran down the right side of his face from his green eyes down to his cheek, giving him the look of a modern-day pirate. The scar on his face and the limp in his leg was the reward he received from chasing after bad guys doing his duty for his country as a Navy SEAL.

Sarah saw the man beneath the scar. She appreciated his kindness to her and her grandfather.

Turning to Dakota, she was aware of his tightened jawline which stayed rigidly in place. He really didn't appreciate that she was giving him more of the tea he so disliked.

Once again, she was reminded of the fact that this man could rival her grandfather for stubbornness. But, she wasn't going to cave in. "I'll be back."

"Sarah, I hope my brother isn't giving you too hard a time." Hunter grinned at his brother and turning winked at Sarah.

She turned to Hunter, squaring her shoulders. "Dakota is as restless as ever, angry at being forced to rest so his leg can heal properly. But, I'm doing my best to help him get better."

"I'll leave the two of you to chat. I'll be back a little later with tea." Sarah nodded at the two brothers and left the room, closing the door behind her.

DAKOTA EYED HIS BROTHER, who looked over at him with a mischievous glitter in his eyes.

"What are you thinking?"

"A moment ago, I noticed how closely you were watching Sarah, brother. Unless I missed my guess, you are quite taken with Angus MacDonald's granddaughter." Hunter sat down in the soft chair near the bed.

Stretching his legs, his steady gaze locked onto Dakota like laser beams as if trying to pin down the truth.

Dakota squirmed uncomfortably. "I'll admit she is attractive. But she is equally infuriating and stubborn."

"Sounds like someone I know." Hunter interrupted, sending him a pointed look.

He nodded and shrugged. "Maybe. But I can assure you she is just as stubborn. As far as anything more, well let's just say it's not like that between us. We're just good friends, nothing more. We have been for years."

He didn't add that the beautiful mountain woman had been on his mind a whole lot lately or that as much as he disliked those herbal medicines she forced him to drink — he liked being near her.

"Oh really?" One of his brother's eyebrows quirked upwards in disbelief. "Then someone should notify Sarah of that fact."

"I get the feeling that she definitely is interested in having more than a friendship with you. It seems to me, you're both doing a one step forward, two steps back dance in this relationship."

Dakota was silent for a moment, as he considered Hunter's words.

"That's probably true. However, she has distanced herself from me, ever since I let her know a few years ago, that I couldn't see myself making a commitment to any woman." Dakota rubbed the back of his neck and sighed at the memory.

"Now, why would you do a fool thing like that?"

Dakota's voice grew impatient. "Because, I don't live a normal life where a wife or a family would be safe. Even at this moment, I'm chomping at the bit to get healed enough, so I can continue searching for the kidnapper in this new case."

"How could I in good conscience bring a woman into that mess?" Dakota grunted his reply, his frustration evident. "I was just telling her the truth, but I didn't mean to hurt her."

"Have you told her that?"

"I didn't lay it out as clear as that."

Hunter shook his head, taking him to task. "Well, I think it's time you did. But, before you do, consider what you're giving up. Sarah is a treasure. Any man would be lucky to have her by his side."

"I can't see myself ever marrying, brother." Fear of Sarah or any woman he cared about getting hurt like his younger sister had been hurt, terrified him.

But, if Dakota was honest, he had avoided this diffi-cult conversation with Sarah for long enough. It was time to pay the piper. "But, I will have that conversation soon."

"I'm glad to hear you agree." Hunter smiled wide and stood to his feet. "Well, it looks like you're doing well enough, despite the nasty leg wound. I'll let Mom know she doesn't need to send in reinforcements."

Dakota grinned.

"I should get going to my ranch. I have some new horses coming in today."

Dakota nodded. "What breed of horses?"

"Quarter horses. I thought to raise them and train them for ranchers around here and across the state of Montana who need good horses for chasing cattle and for rodeos. So, I continue the search for high quality Quarter horses."

"Well, you have always loved that breed of horses. I remember Dad sometimes called you the horse whisperer. He said you seemed to have a closer connection to horses than the rest of us."

Hunter smiled softly. "Yeah, Dad did say that. Not sure if that's true, but I try my best to understand them."

"When I'm feeling better, I'll need to stop by and take a look at what you've got going on at your ranch."

"You do that." Hunter walked to the door, before turning. "And let me know if there's anything else you need."

Dakota thought for a moment before responding. "Could you ask Sheriff Turnbull to stop by? I need to talk to him. There are some details of what happened that he'll want to know."

"Sure." Hunter eyed him. "Anything else?"

"Yeah, one more thing. Could you bring Sarge here? I find I'm missing that fur-ball." Dakota gave his brother a side-ways smile.

"I can see why. Your dog has already won the rest of the family over to his way of thinking." Hunter grinned. "Our nephews are going to miss him, but I will bring him over."

"Thanks, Hunter. See you." A small smile lifted the corners of Dakota's lips as his brother left.

Restlessness hit him once more. He needed to get well in a hurry. There was so much that needed to get done.

Gingerly, he pulled his legs over the side of the bed and stood to his feet.

His legs were wobbly, but he took comfort in the fact

that he was standing, even if it was mostly on his good leg. He was desperate to heal up as fast as possible.

"Dakota, it will take some time to get your leg muscles back to normal. Take it easy, son and let your body heal." Doctor Weston walked into his room, his black medical bag in hand.

Sighing, Dakota sat down on the bed. Unexpectedly, his body shivered and he struggled to pull his legs underneath the bedcovers.

Doctor Weston helped him get settled and after checking his vitals and cleaning the wounded leg, he assured Dakota that all was healing nicely.

"I'll be back tomorrow. But your wound continues to heal well. Rest is what your body needs most of all right now." Doctor Weston nodded at both of them and picking up his medical bag, left.

Dakota was still wincing in pain from all the movement, when Sarah stepped into the room. Her green eyes locked onto his, noticing his struggle.

He shifted uncomfortably under the weight of her scrutiny. Did she feel sorry for him? Compassion he could allow, but any sort of pity he would not.

Sarah handed him the tea.

Reluctantly he sipped from the hot liquid and winced.

Forcing a smile, he took another drink looking into her beautiful green eyes.

His gaze took in all of her lovely features and an awareness of his childhood friend increased ten-fold.

A thick strawberry blond braid hung down to her waist and shifted with every movement of her slender body. Her hair shone like honey and looked to be as smooth as silk. Was it as soft as he imagined?

As she stepped closer to pull the blankets up his shivering body, the unruly braid in question fell over her shoulder and landed on his arm. It was like a whisper of silk against his skin.

He began to move his hand to touch it again, but she quickly moved the long braid behind her back.

"Sorry. My hair seems to have a mind of its own."

He watched her cheeks turn pink and thought she looked even more adorable. "I don't mind. Your hair is long and beautiful and smells like roses. It was my mother's favorite scent too."

Now what was he doing, spilling his innermost thoughts like that? Ever since he'd talked with his brother earlier, he couldn't stop thinking about Sarah.

Dakota decided he'd better keep a tighter rein on his tongue from here on out. He couldn't afford to let messy emotions get in the way of what he was supposed to do.

Sarah's cheeks turned a lovely shade of pink at his compliment. "Thank you. Roses are my favorite scent."

Dakota was about to reply, when suddenly a loud banging was heard on the cabin door.

Maisie barked loudly, limping towards the kitchen where grandfather could be heard talking with someone.

Sarah hurried over to the door and opened it slightly.

A booming male voice thundered through the cabin. "Angus, we made a deal and I've come to collect on your promise."

"What promise was that?"

"You gave me your word that you'd give me something

you prized greatly if I won that card game over a month ago."

"Well, I am a man of my word." Angus's voice sounded irritated.

"But, I haven't received anything from you. Perhaps, you were so sure of yourself, that you didn't think you'd lose?" A loud chuckle echoed around the small cabin. "But like it or not, today I'm here to collect my prize."

Angus sighed. "Aye, then. I suppose it's time. I'll get my coat. You can take my favorite black Holstein cow with you this very day."

"No, it's not the cow I want." The man bellowed loudly.

"What? Well, what do you want then?"

Dakota motioned for Sarah to open the door wider so he could hear what was being said.

Carefully she pushed the door further open, leaning against the wall so she wouldn't be seen.

They listened as the gruff male voice continued. "I figure, since I've waited so long, it is my right to choose another prize."

The man's voice sounded slurred. "I've decided I want your granddaughter as my wife. That's the prize I want and that's the prize I mean to claim."

Dakota looked over at Sarah who stood as still as a statue. Her face turned ashen and her hand shook on the doorknob she was holding.

Her green eyes were wide in fear and her fingers turned white as they gripped the doorknob.

CHAPTER FOUR

arah

SARAH SHRUNK a little more on the inside with each angry demand that spewed out of the mountain man's lips.

A shiver escaped her lips and her body shuddered. His jarring tones sent a violent shiver down her back, and with it came terrible memories.

Her stepfather had made demands of her too. In fact, he had insisted she obey him, by whatever means necessary.

"You'd better do as I say girl and hurry up with those dishes, or you'll be sorry." Her stepfather guzzled down his fourth bottle of beer that evening. He was already staggering unsteadily as he walked from the kitchen to his sofa to watch television in their small living room.

She knew when he was this drunk he was at his most dangerous. She needed to hurry.

Her little hands reached for the large plate. Grabbing the dishcloth scrubbed the spaghetti stains off the plate. Rinsing each dish under the tap water, she quickly set them on the drying rack.

In record time she dried the dishes and put them away. She didn't want to do anything to make her stepfather even angrier. Her arms were still purple from the last beating he gave her.

"Now go to your room and don't come out until morning."
She ran to her small bedroom, closed the door and cried on her pillow. Why could she never do anything right? Why did her stepfather hate her so much? All she longed for was to belong somewhere and to be loved.

"Sarah." She heard the soft male voice in her ear. She jerked her head up at the sound. The memories that haunted her still, faded into the background as he repeated her name.

"Sarah?" Turning her head, she saw Dakota standing near her, crutches under his arms.

Swallowing quickly, she nodded. Her voiced sounded raw and stilted. "Sorry. My mind was somewhere else. What did you say?"

She did her best to clear her emotions from the vivid images that showed up unexpectedly in her memory.

Fergus Drummond's loud insistence that she marry him, had reminded her of her abusive stepfather and it scared her. Her biggest fear was to be forced again under the control of a man who was drunk, abusive and demanding.

A furrow formed between his brows and his dark eyes

settled on hers like a searchlight intent on finding all her secrets.

Sarah looked down at her shaky hands for a moment, in an effort to hide how vulnerable she felt from his gaze. She didn't want him to know all her embarrassing secrets.

"I was asking if you knew this man?" Dakota tilted his head towards the open doorway, as the loud argument continued between the two men.

Sarah's gaze followed Dakota's and she caught a glimpse of the stocky mountain man with the scraggily dark brown hair and beard.

Turning back to Dakota, she nodded. "Fergus Drummond. He's a neighbor."

"Well, he's an extremely rude neighbor who sounds like he's had far too much to drink." The argument between the two men in the other room continued.

"Maybe I should join your grandfather and encourage your neighbor to leave." Dakota stepped towards the door, but Sarah gently placed her hand on his arm.

She shook her head. "I know you mean well, but I think we should let grandfather handle him. He will make sure Fergus Drummond goes soon."

Her grandfather had always protected her, especially from unwanted advances from men. Besides, Dakota was still wounded and she wouldn't be able to live with herself if somehow he got hurt again, or worse.

Dakota nodded. "All right. If you're sure."

The loud argument continued between the men in the other room.

"No. I won't allow you to claim my granddaughter as your wife. My Sarah isn't part of our deal." Sarah heard the anger in her grandfather's voice and knew he'd reached the end of his patience with their uncouth neighbor.

"But, I wasn't to know that, now was I?" Fergus Drummond blustered and moved unsteadily on his feet. "So, I say the deal stands and I get to choose my prize. And I choose Sarah to be my wife."

Fergus continued to make his loud demands known to her grandfather.

Sarah's body shivered with a mixture of anger and fear.

All of a sudden, a strong arm wrapped around her waist, pulling her close. With one hand Dakota gripped her waist and with the other, he steadied himself with the crutches.

"It will be okay. I've got you." His whispered. She could feel the warmth of his breath against her ear.

She shivered at the tenderness in his touch and in his voice.

Despite the fact that Sarah had warm tingles going up and down her spine from being in the arms of her childhood friend, she needed to move away from him.

Annoyed with herself, Sarah admitted there was a big part of her that wanted to stay in his protective embrace.

But, that wasn't a good idea.

Dakota had been her best friend for years. He had made it plain a few years ago that he wasn't interested in a committed relationship.

Sarah had quickly learned that lesson the last time she went out of her way to help care for him. She wouldn't put her heart so easily on the line again.

The memory of her grandmother's wise words from years ago popped into her mind. She had just turned eighteen and Dakota had been back from the police academy and stopped by for a visit.

After he left, her grandmother spoke softly. *Sarah darling, I can see that you have feelings for Dakota that go beyond friendship. I know he admires you, but I feel like he's closed himself off to love for some reason. I sense in him deep pain that needs to be mended before he can truly love a woman. This might take some time, my dear.*

She didn't give much thought to her grandmother's words at the time. However, now years later Sarah realized the wisdom and foresight of her Grandmother's words.

Her heart had already been battered one too many times throughout life. She wasn't willing to repeat that.

Quickly, she stepped out of his arms. Sarah caught a glimpse of his questioning gaze, before she turned and moved closer to the doorway.

She desperately needed to distance herself from him. It was much too difficult to be so close to the man she still loved.

Glad for the distraction, she turned to look through the slightly open door trying to see what was going on in the other room.

Loud arguing continued between both men.

Sarah gasped as her grandfather grew red in the face and marched towards the front door and opened it with a loud thump.

"It's time for you to get out of my house. Now." Grandfather's voice was loud and angry. "I believe your brain has been muddled by all that strong drink. Listen to me closely. I refuse to give my granddaughter to you to marry."

Sarah stepped out of the room just in time to see her grandfather hurrying after their neighbor. "It's time you left Fergus. You're not welcome here any longer."

She rushed to the front door and saw her grandfather leading his favorite cow by a rope.

Fergus jumped onto the saddle of his horse and grabbing the rope he trotted off with the cow barely managing to keep up.

As Sarah watched from the doorway, she was relieved when their neighbor finally disappeared down the dirt road.

Grandfather wheeled around, hurrying towards the fence for the cows, when suddenly he tripped and fell.

"Ah..." Grandfather's pain-filled voice ripped through the air. Sarah ran towards him.

Reaching him, she kneeled on the ground looking into his white upturned face.

"Grandfather, what's wrong?" Sarah watched as he gripped his leg. "What happened?"

"I tripped over that log and twisted my leg something fierce. I can't move it without pain."

Sarah was thinking about what they should do, when she heard Dakota speak.

"We'll help get you back into the house, Angus." Dakota limped over and grabbed Angus under his shoulder and Sarah did the same.

They were able to slowly get Angus inside the house and lifted him onto his bed.

Dakota limped out of the room while Sarah stayed to see her grandfather settled.

"I'm glad Fergus Drummond is gone. He scares me, grandfather." Sarah swallowed, trying to get rid of the shakiness in her voice.

Grandfather shook his head, the furrow in his forehead growing deeper. "I know Sarah, and I'm sorry." He rubbed his forehead. "Problem is, he's not likely to give up anytime soon."

Sighing, Sarah handed her grandfather a glass of water and an aspirin. "Perhaps, we should move to town. That way we'd be far away from him."

"Sarah, my dear. There will be strange folks wherever we live." Grandfather shook his head, a familiar determination in his jawline. "No, my first priority is to see that you are settled. Then maybe I'll consider moving. But, not before."

"I understand, Grandfather." Sarah squeezed his hand hoping to calm his agitation. "I'll call Dr. Weston to come take a look at your leg. Meanwhile, drink a little water and try to rest."

"I shouldn't rest. I need to take care of feeding the cattle and chickens." Her grandfather's forehead puckered with misery.

"Don't worry. I can feed the animals. I've been helping you for years, haven't I?" Sarah sent him a warm smile and pushed back a gray curl from his forehead.

Grandfather nodded. "I'll rest easier knowing my animals are taken care of."

"I know you will. Rest now." Sarah leaned over and kissed his forehead.

She walked out of her grandfather's bedroom and called the doctor. Happy that the doctor said he would be over soon, Sarah walked over to Dakota's room and knocked on the door.

"Come in." Dakota's low voice called out.

Sarah walked in the door, to see him sitting on the bed reading over some notes.

"Can I talk to you for a minute?" Nervously, Sarah threaded her fingers through the long braid that hung over one shoulder.

His dark eyes peered at her over the papers in his hand. "Sure. What's up?"

Sarah swallowed, a little hesitant to speak what was on her mind. She was likely to shock him, but she figured it was the only way forward.

"I'm worried about my grandfather."

He nodded. "That's understandable. But, the doctor will know how to set his leg properly."

"I know. It's not his leg, that worries me."

"Oh?" He looked at her, a question lingering in his gaze.

Sarah looked down and clasped her hands together in front of her for a moment. "Yes. As you know he's hurt himself today. And I worry that as he gets older, it's getting more difficult for him to continue to live here on the mountain."

She explained. "I've asked him to consider moving to town, but he won't hear of it. Grandfather says he won't budge until he sees me settled. And by settled, what he means is married."

Heat crept up her neck to her cheeks. She didn't really

want to talk to Dakota about this subject. But, what choice did she have? There was no one else to whom she could go to for help.

Sarah had come this far, so she might as well bulldoze her way forward. "So I've come up with an idea."

"I'm listening." His dark eyes studied her.

She swallowed nervously. With a shaky hand she tucked a loose blond curl behind one ear. "Well, it's like this. I believe we can help each other. You're searching for the little girl that's gone missing. If she's anywhere on this mountain or near our town — I can help. I know this area like the back of my hand."

He nodded. "That's true. In return what do you want?"

"If you agree to a fake marriage with me, then my grandfather will be happy that I'm settled and would consider moving to town." Sarah could see his eyes widened at her words.

Her idea must have surprised him, because he didn't speak for a few minutes.

"A fake marriage? I don't know if my mother would be able to swallow that idea." Dakota rubbed the back of his neck.

"Well, I was thinking about that. Maybe for the sake of your mother and my grandfather, we could pretend that we married for love when we're around them. Somehow we could convince them that this marriage is real." Sarah talked quickly, nervousness overcoming her.

This idea sounded crazy, she knew. But, it was the only way that she could think of, to help her grandfather.

She continued. "With my grandfather's bad leg, he's

going to need extra care. But, he still won't consider moving."

Dakota grimaced. "Not to mention your crazy neighbor who seems determined to carry you off and marry you."

Heat flamed her cheeks as she thought of Fergus Drummond demanding to marry her. What was he thinking?

"I don't know what he was thinking. He had too much to drink, that much was clear." Sarah shook her head, looking down at her braid, embarrassed at the day's turn of events.

Dakota sighed. "Well Sarah, I have an idea of what he was thinking. You're a beautiful woman."

She looked up, surprised by his compliment. For Dakota — who was a man of few words — he could string some words of appreciation together when he put his mind to it.

She was surprised that he felt that way about her. "Thank you Dakota. That's nice of you to say."

"Welcome." He rubbed the back of his neck. It was a sure sign something troubled him. "But, I'm not sure about this idea of yours, Sarah."

"I know, it seems far-fetched and a little crazy. But I'm desperate. I'll do whatever it takes so my grandfather will be cared for. And like you pointed out, it will also put a stop Fergus Drummond from trying to marry me." Nervously, she bit her lip. "Will you think about it?"

Dakota nodded. "I will consider your idea. But, give me a day or two to think about it, okay?"

"Sure. Thank you." With a quick nod, Sarah offered a wobbly smile and hurried out of his room.

As she hurried outside to feed the cattle, she couldn't help but hope that Dakota would agree to her idea.

❧

A FAKE MARRIAGE? Dakota had thought about Sarah's idea and tossed and turned most of the night because of it.

Once again, he remembered the rule he'd made earlier on in his career. He would never place the woman he loved in danger. The best way to do that, was to commit to never marry.

After losing a much beloved sister and later watching his mom suffer because of that heart-rending loss, he never wanted to risk any woman he loved.

With his work as a Private Investigator chasing kidnappers and other offenders, he was convinced anyone he loved would be an easy target.

Dakota sighed. He would need to tell Sarah he couldn't offer her a fake marriage.

A sudden knock on his door, brought him out of his reverie.

Sarah opened the door. "Someone's here to see you."

Dakota nodded. "Thanks."

Sheriff Turnbull stepped into the room. The tall, gray-haired man, looked him over and grinned. "So, you've been holed up here on the mountain? Seems like a nice spot."

"My staying here wasn't by choice, as you know. My leg is almost healed, then I'll be back on the case."

Sheriff Turnbull removed his cowboy hat and sat down on the chair near the bed. "I had two officers investigate what happened the day you were shot."

He ran a hand through his hair and sighed. "They questioned two hunters who were spotted near the area that day. However, the two men had witnesses who saw them shoot the deer."

"My officers also talked with a couple of folks who lived on the mountain including an old miner who said he shot an animal that day, but stated he didn't think there was any person out near his cabin."

A shadow of annoyance crossed Dakota's face. "So, there's no answers for who shot at me?"

"Not yet. We'll keep looking into it, don't worry. We will find out who is responsible." Sheriff Turnbull replied, his voice firm and final.

Dakota nodded, expelling a breath in relief. "Good."

The Sheriff shifted in chair. "Now, tell me what you have so far on this kidnapping case."

"When I was first asked to search for Mindy, I was at her parents home in Colorado and I discovered details that led me here to Refuge Mountain. A set of matches that was in the flower bed, a used cigarette, and a boot print. Recognize this place?" Dakota held up a set of matches with the name of a business printed on the front.

"Harry's Bar and Grill? Yeah, that's on the south side of town. That watering hole has all sorts of strange customers. You think the kidnapper showed up there?"

"Yeah, I do. Why else would these matches — from our small town in Montana — be found in the flower bed at the missing girl's home in Colorado?"

"Hmm. I see your point." Sheriff Turnbull nodded. "And your other discovery?"

"This." Dakota held up his smartphone with a photo of a large boot print in the dirt. There was an imprint of a large star that was embedded into the ground near a patch of flowers.

"Well, that certainly is a unique boot print."

Dakota nodded. "My assistant did some research and came up with only a couple of possibilities. One is a boot that used to be made for members of the military and the other is from a shoe company that creates a sturdy boot, worn by miners or heavy laborers."

"Well, that narrows down the list of possible suspects. But we'll need a lot more details to find the kidnapper." Sheriff put his hat back on. "I wish there would have been more evidence on whoever shot you. As it stands, we really don't have a lot of information."

"I thought as much. Looks like I'll need to put on my P.I. hat and do some searching around."

Sheriff nodded. "Do that. If you want to get some real answers from the folks at Harry's Bar and Grill, take a woman with you. You'll catch more flies with honey than with vinegar."

Dakota nodded with a grin. "Duly noted."

The Sheriff stood to his feet. "It's time I got going. I'm needed at the office. I hope you'll be on your feet soon, son." Sheriff tipped his hat and left.

Dakota thought on what the Sheriff had said about taking a woman with him.

After the Sheriff left, he searched through his backpack looking through the documents that he had brought with him, so he could finish his research.

Pulling out a stack of papers, he looked through them one by one until his gaze landed on an open envelope.

The letter from his dad. Mack Callahan's familiar bold handwriting was scrawled on top of the front of the envelope.

He had read the letter from his father when he passed away a couple years ago.

However, the memory of what was written inside was hazy and Dakota felt the need to read his dad's words again. Opening the letter, he began to read.

For my son Dakota.

If you're reading this letter, it's because I've gone to my reward.

But, I've had a good life with a wonderful family.

Family has always been the most important thing in our home. Your mother and I were thrilled the day we found you in that foster home years ago.

That moment is still as real now as if it happened yesterday.

You stood looking at us proud of your heritage and as fierce as any warrior at seven years old. I knew then, who you'd be when you grew up.

There were scars. Sure, you had a few wounds on the outside, but most of your scars were on the inside from a family that was taken from you too soon.

I could see a lot of pain hidden in those dark eyes of yours — pain and heartache that no child of that young age should understand. Even though your eyes held pain that day, you still agreed to let us take you to our home.

You became our son, and you bore the Callahan name with

respect and pride. Your mother and I have often thought of that first year when you and your seven brothers came into our family. Each of you boys brought us great joy, and we've loved being your parents.

Son, many times throughout your childhood and even these few years as an adult, you have shown an ability to have great insight into people and who they really are.

I know your brothers value that quality in you. Especially, your connection with your brother Levi (may he rest in peace). You two connected strongly, even though you each were from a different heritage.

But, you became fast friends and brothers. When Levi died on a military mission a few years ago, I believe it broke your heart most of all. I'm sorry for that, Dakota. You've already had more than your share of heartache.

But, it's because of the unique way you see details about people, that I want to ask you to do something for me.

Dakota, I'm asking that despite the differences of opinion you've had with Sarah MacDonald in the past, that you make it your priority to try to understand and help Sarah and her grandfather.

Show up to help her for two months. Help her to take care of their cattle and chickens and fix things up around Angus MacDonald's small mountain ranch.

Ever since her grandmother passed away, I believe it's been difficult for Angus as well as Sarah. The only family she has left in the world, is her grandfather.

One word of warning: I have reason to believe her stepfather will be released from jail soon and will likely try to reconnect with Sarah.

That's where you come in. I believe you could be there to

protect her. Being close to Sarah, could also give you the time needed to heal some old wounds between the two of you.

Who knows, but maybe helping Sarah will bring the two of you together? It's possible that the two of you might fall in love once again.

It would be your second chance at a happy life with the woman you loved years ago, much like I had with your mother. Besides, a Christmas wedding would be the perfect way to end the year.

I understand what I'm asking you is a difficult task, but I know you can do this.

You're a fine man, son. You're tough from all that you've endured, but I know inside you beats the heart of a compassionate and caring man.

If you agree to help Sarah for two months — and my faithful lawyer Mr. McCrae agrees that you have — then you will receive ten million dollars and a share (along with your six brothers) in the Callahan Manufacturing Company in Refuge Mountain.

The amount of money from both, should give you a good start on funding your dream.

I wish I could be a fly on the wall to watch you marry and live your dreams, but Doc says my time on this earth is short.

So instead, it looks like I'll be cheering you on from up above. Remember, I'm proud of you, son. I love you, Dad.

Dakota swallowed back emotion. His hands shook as he folded the letter and slipped it back inside the envelope.

He'd forgotten about the letter from his father.

It was encouraging to read his dad's words written by

his own hand. He was surprised again, by how much his dad believed in him.

A shiver of warmth swirled in his belly and he smiled pensively, missing his dad more than ever.

His thoughts shifted to Levi. All that his father had said was true. The two of them had been brothers, but they were more than that. They had been best friends.

Dakota had tried to talk Levi out of signing up for boot camp, but he had insisted. His brother told him, he wanted to do his duty. He promised he would only do one tour.

That one tour of duty had ended his life, far too soon.

A dull ache sat like lead at the pit of Dakota's stomach as he remembered his brother.

He missed Levi. He supposed his father had been right to steer his thoughts towards someone he could help… *someone like Sarah.*

Dakota sighed as his thoughts turned to his beautiful childhood friend.

It annoyed him, that his dad was matchmaking even from beyond the grave. Even going as far as to hint at a Christmas wedding.

Problem was, getting married wasn't what he wanted. On the other hand, he did want to protect Sarah.

If Sarah's stepfather did return anytime soon, Dakota wanted to make sure, that cruel man didn't hurt Sarah any longer.

He would need to stay close by her side in order to protect her.

Maybe, Sarah's idea of a fake marriage between them, wasn't so crazy after all.

CHAPTER FIVE

Sarah

Nervously, Sarah opened her bedroom door and walked out towards the living room.

"My granddaughter and her new husband will be moving…" Angus MacDonald stopped mid-sentence in a conversation with the new cook Dakota had hired and looked up.

His gray eyes widened. A warm smile soon followed.

"Lass, you are a beautiful bride. Your grandmother would be so pleased to see you wearing her wedding dress on this very special day." Grandfather's Scottish brogue got thicker during more emotional moments. A tell-tale shimmer moistened his eyes.

Sarah felt the warmth of his love from across the room and she hurried over to give him a hug. "I'm grateful that you encouraged me to wear grandmother's wedding dress. It means the world to me. Thank you, grandfather."

Sarah stepped back and slipped her hands into his. As she looked into those familiar gray eyes, she smiled and asked. "Will I do?"

"Ah, my lovely Sarah. You will more than do — you will shine on your wedding day." Grandfather leaned over and kissed her cheek.

When he held out his arm, Sarah grinned and slipped her hand into the crook of his arm.

Grandfather's cook hurried ahead of them and opened the front door to the cabin.

"You look lovely, Sarah." Mrs. Moore was a sixty-year-old widow whom Dakota had hired to take care of her grandfather. She also happened to be a nurse.

She had been worried about her grandfather when Dakota first suggested they move to the cabin on his ranch land. She had been very uncomfortable about leaving her grandfather alone.

He had seen her worry for her grandfather and offered to hire someone who would be willing to be both cook and nurse.

It eased her mind to know that her grandfather would have someone to watch out for him, since she could no longer be there for him.

Mrs. Moore had only been with them for a couple of days, but already Sarah was convinced the widow was exactly the person her grandfather needed.

Sarah was very grateful to her new husband for his generosity.

It had taken a bit of coaxing to get grandfather to agree to have a nurse stay with him.

But in the end, he agreed.

Sarah was thankful for peace of mind knowing her grandfather would be cared for. It was a gift that she desperately needed.

She walked out the door and down the steps, her grip tightened on her grandfather's arm as Sarah saw her husband-to-be waiting for her.

Dakota stood motionless beside the pastor as he watched her walk slowly towards him on the green grass.

Sarah felt a little intimidated by Dakota's large family. She had been an only child and her dad had died suddenly when she was still a small child.

Her mom married her stepdad but then she died of cancer when Sarah was only five years old. A large family was something she longed for, but had never had a chance to experience.

Now she would finally have her turn.

She was happy to be part of the Callahan family, even if it was only for a short while.

After all, this was a fake marriage with a precise end in mind.

Guilt tightened her belly. Both, her grandfather and Dakota's mother believed the two of them were marrying for love. They were convinced this marriage was real.

Her hands shook as her grandfather gently placed her hand in Dakota's much larger one.

Nervously, she tilted her head to look up at him. His dark eyes stared at her with an intensity she'd never seen before.

The pastor began speaking, but it seemed as if she was hearing the words in the background. She was so focused on the man she was to marry.

Dakota's hooded gaze watched her closely.

What was he thinking? Did he regret his decision to go through with this marriage-in-name-only?

The pastor's words interrupted her thoughts. "Do you take this woman to be your lawfully wedded wife?"

Dakota responded, his voice cool and steady. "I do."

Sarah swallowed at the calm and bold confidence in his voice.

The question was repeated to her.

With a wobbly voice Sarah softly answered. "I do."

The pastor looked at Dakota and with a smile said. "You may kiss your bride."

Her cheeks turned pink and she swallowed, feeling flustered.

Dakota had only kissed her once, but afterwards he seemed to regret it.

After that day, he left her alone. To this day, she felt the sting of his rejection. Was there something she had done wrong?

She wanted their relationship to grow into something more, but it wasn't to be.

After that kiss, things changed between them.

Dakota wasn't his usual carefree self with her as he had been in the past. Not since that day.

He had always had a determination about him once he decided something. And it seemed he had decided to avoid her.

For Sarah, that fierce determination that he had in spades, was both honorable and frustrating all at the same time.

Today on her wedding day, she would finally be kissed by this man once more. A shy anticipation spread to every cell in her body.

Dakota's eyes darkened as his gaze met hers and then fell to her lips.

With gentle hands on her shoulders, he pulled her close. He gently touched her cheek with the back of his fingers, while his unwavering gaze met hers.

She shivered at his gentle touch.

Slowly he lowered his head and touched his lips to hers.

The sweetness of his kiss, left her breathless in wonder.

Sarah didn't want Dakota's kiss to end.

Enfolded in her new husband's arms she felt the safest she'd ever been. Not just safe but peaceful. Beyond that she felt loved.

Now that she'd said I do, he was her husband and she wanted to go on kissing him forever. Her breath stilled as Dakota's mouth captured hers fully. Nipping and pulling his mouth caressed hers.

His warm lips molded against hers until she didn't know where his ended and hers began.

Her heart shuddered away in her ears like a loose wheel.

It was as if he had branded her, making her his.

Her legs melted and she tightened her grip on his

arms. Her knees weakened like jelly. Her heart went ninety. And her lips tingled with the warmth of his kisses.

Sarah felt like she was floating on soft white clouds. It was a beautiful feeling. A feeling so wonderful that she never wanted it to end.

❦

IN SPITE of his vow to keep his distance, Dakota couldn't resist holding his new wife in his arms.

With one hand he gently ran his fingers through her thick blond hair, before sweeping the silky tendrils away from her face.

Slowly, he bent downwards, pressing his lips to hers.

As his lips touched hers, he released a soft sigh.

His bride tasted of strawberries. Sweetly soft, exactly as he remembered.

Pulling Sarah closer, he deepened their kiss, longing for more of her sweet kisses.

He'd waited years for this moment.

The desire he had for Sarah was more than simply a friend, it was a secret he'd kept hidden for a long time.

Dakota had chosen a self-imposed strict set of rules ever since he began training at the Police Academy.

One of the decisions he'd made early on, was not to allow himself to get serious about any woman.

That meant casual dates only.

No commitments. No long-term entanglements. No falling in love.

Yet in spite of himself, he had yearned for a relationship with Sarah. He'd first really begun to notice his childhood friend, the day he graduated from the Police Academy.

Dakota had arrived back home for a few days, before beginning his new job as an FBI agent. He had been hauling more hay to feed the cattle in the far pasture, when he found Sarah stuck on the side of the road in her grandfather's old truck.

She had been returning home from a quilting bee with some of her friends at *A Goode Yarn*. It was a special weekly time the owner of the store — Lynda Goode — had been willing to reserve for the quilters in their community.

But, Sarah's truck had a flat tire. He saw her struggling and got out of his truck and began to fix it. She was relieved by his help. In no time at all, he had replaced the flat tire with the spare one.

He remembered, as soon as he'd finished fixing the tire, thunder had cracked in the sky above. Sarah's eyes widened in fear and she jerked visibly at the deafening sound.

He didn't really know why he reached for her, except that she looked so afraid. He comforted her by whispering soothing words in her ear and soon her trembling stopped. But, when he pulled away, he couldn't resist kissing her sweet lips.

Those memories surged through him, as once again he held beautiful Sarah in his arms... but this time she was his wife.

Suddenly, a greater awareness came to him of what it would mean to be a married man.

He was responsible for his wife's protection and wanted to do everything he could to add to her happiness.

The problem was, he couldn't see a positive outcome for them. He had failed to deliver the protection and happiness his mother and sister desperately needed years earlier.

How could he hope that he might achieve the impossible now with his new wife?

Forcing himself to step away from Sarah, Dakota stood perfectly still despite the somersaults circling his stomach. A pang of regret hit him, as large green eyes filled with confusion stared back at him.

Gazing down at his new bride, he pushed away the fear that he liked her kisses a little too much. She looked up and Dakota imagined himself nibbling on her bottom lip once more. The need to haul her back into his arms and kiss her again, nearly sent him to the brink of his control.

He sent her a lopsided grin, then smiled at the wedding guests as they were officially introduced as husband and wife.

Swallowing back emotion, he clasped her hand in his.

Soon they were surrounded by warm hugs and enthusiastic congratulations from family members.

"Son, I'm so happy for you and Sarah." He pulled his mother into a warm embrace.

She stepped back with moisture in her eyes and a smile on her beautiful face. "Your father would be so pleased. Before he died, your dad said he was convinced you and Sarah would find love together once again. I'm sure he's smiling down on us today."

"That's a nice thought, mom." Dakota was grateful for his mom's cheerful words; he couldn't help but feel like the biggest con artist around.

He had managed to deceive his mom into believing this marriage was real. Not only that, but she was convinced they were in love.

Somehow, he would need to do what he could to make this marriage to his childhood friend seem as real as possible, at least to his mother and Sarah's grandfather.

And yet, in the middle of it he would need to keep his heart intact. How was he going to do that?

As family and friends came to offer their congratulations, Dakota stood next to his bride feeling uncomfortable as his own emotions stirred strongly.

Emotions like feeling pride and happiness that Sarah was a Callahan now. These sentiments were unfamiliar to him, yet in this moment they felt so right.

His gaze drifted over to his wife, thinking how beautiful she looked with her cheeks' stained pink.

Living with Sarah over the next few months worried him. Just how was he going to keep his heart from falling for his fake wife?

***

Sara watched as Annie Callahan talked with Dakota. Her new husband talked with his mother and joked with his brothers. He had been kind to everyone else.

Yet, she could tell Dakota was tense. Sarah wished she knew what he was thinking. In spite of the strain of the day, he had definitely played his part today, acting like a man marrying for love.

Heat spread up her neck to her cheeks, her heartbeat accelerated.

Tiny butterflies that began with Dakota's kiss were still tickling her belly.

She'd enjoyed his care and attention a little too much today. That's what worried her. How would she keep her heart from becoming too deeply involved with her husband? Sarah didn't know how she would manage that, but she needed to try.

Dakota's mom finished talking to her husband and moved toward her. She did her best to calm her strained nerves.

"It's so good to see a young couple in love." Annie Callahan placed her hands in Sarah's and gently squeezed. "Sarah, that wedding dress is beautiful on you."

"Thank you. It was my grandmother's wedding dress from over fifty years ago. I'm grateful grandfather let me wear it today." Sarah swallowed back emotion as she thought of her grandmother and mother who had passed away far too soon.

"I'm sorry your mother and grandmother couldn't be here to see how beautiful you look on your wedding day, my dear. It's very difficult to go through those mixed emotions on your special day. Perhaps, I can help in some small way." Annie Callahan had always been a gentle and caring soul.

"You already have helped me so much, simply by listening and caring." Sarah squeezed her new mother-in-law's hands. "It means the world to me. Thank you, Mrs. Callahan."

"Oh, please call me Annie, or mom would be even better." Annie winked at her, leaned closer and spoke in a half whisper. "I'd love if you called me mom, more than anything in the world."

"I'd be pleased to call you Mom." Sarah's mouth curved into a smile.

Sarah swallowed back tears that threatened to spill over. It would be a wonderful gift to have a mom in her life once more, even if it was for only a short time.

It had been much too long since she had known the gentle touch of a mother. Annie was kind and compassionate and she looked amazing. When Annie smiled, tiny crows feet appeared by her eyes. She was beautiful.

"Calling me mom would make me happier than anything. I've been waiting for another daughter to join our family." Annie hugged her.

"I'm glad." Embraced in the warm cocoon of her new mother's arms, she wanted this feeling to last forever. She longed for years to once again feel the love of a mother.

So great was her longing, that she pushed back the reminder that this marriage wasn't real.

Her and Dakota had agreed to have a fake marriage so that her grandfather would consider moving to town and also so that Dakota could have her help finding the missing girl.

She needed to remember that. Although, with all the love she'd been shown today from Dakota's family, she really wanted to be part of the Callahan family for good.

Inwardly, she winced in regret for deceiving her kind

mother-in-law about the reasons for her son's marriage to her.

Sarah was sure this wouldn't be the first time her conscience would prick her.

It was clear, Annie Callahan believed their fake marriage was very real and that her son was in love. Sarah would need to be careful not to cause her new mother-in-law any reason to doubt her and Dakota's love for each other.

Before long, all wedding guests sat down at the small tables that had been setup on the lawn in front of the cabin. Soon, the caterers brought food to the tables.

Dakota had hired caterers to take care of the meal and he'd taken care of the music. It had been on very short notice, but his mother had recommended a small catering business who said they could do it. Sarah had been surprised that Dakota had managed to get all the details organized so quickly.

As Sarah sat at the table, her two new sisters, Abby and Sierra, joined her as well as Sarah's good friend CoraLee.

Abby held her little girl on her lap who was napping at the moment.

"What a perfect picture you make holding your little girl close to your heart, Abby." Sarah smiled at her new sister-in-law.

Abby smiled wide, her green eyes dancing. "Well, it might look perfect at the moment, but just wait until she wakes up. This little one keeps me busy."

Sierra giggled. "I think this baby will most likely be active too. The way he or she is smashing the daylights out of my ribcage, might be a sign of things to come."

"Do you know your baby's gender?" Sarah asked.

Sierra shook her head. "No, Denver wanted to be surprised. Since I would have a difficult time keeping it a secret from him, I chose not to have the doctor tell me. But we're excited and can't wait to hold this little one in our arms."

Sarah sighed with a smile. "That will be a wonderful moment."

Sierra peered over at Sarah, her eyes full of teasing. "Who knows, maybe it won't be too long until you and Dakota have a baby of your own."

Sarah swallowed, knowing that their fake marriage arrangement would make that impossible. She couldn't tell them the truth however, so she settled for a vague answer. "I guess we'll see."

The hot meal that the caterers brought over to each table, was delicious.

Since Abby and Sierra were talking with each other, Sarah was glad to have a moment to chat with her friend.

"I'm glad you were back in town for a while and could come to my wedding, CoraLee." Sarah whispered.

"You know I wouldn't miss it for the world." Her friend squeezed her hand giving her a big smile.

Sarah grinned. "I'm glad. You are as beautiful ever. How's modeling life treating you in the big city of Paris?"

Roses stained her friend's cheeks as she responded. "It's been exciting to be in the most romantic city in the world for the past couple of years. I've met so many interesting people and have made more money than I ever have as a model."

"Yet, I can't help but feel homesick. It's been such a

long time since I've seen my family and have been able to talk with friends like you, Sarah."

Sarah could hear the sadness in her friend's voice. "I'm sorry. It must be difficult to be away from home for months at a time."

CoraLee nodded. "Yes, it is. But let's not talk about me, I want to hear about you. Let's take this wedding for example. Your marriage to Dakota seemed to happen real fast."

Her friend had been the one person to whom Sarah shared the details of their marriage-of-convenience. "I already told you. This is a marriage that will be convenient for both of us. We've agreed to help one another."

Her friend, shook her head silently. "I thought people did that sort of thing a hundred years ago, but not nowadays."

"It's not usually done nowadays, that's true. But, sometimes a person needs to do something unusual to get what they really want." Sarah took a sip of her water, peering over at her friend.

CoraLee looked thoughtful. "I suppose that's true. Well, I really hope this works out well for you both. If he ends up breaking your heart, he'll have to answer to me."

Sarah grinned at her friend. CoraLee had always been her defender and a trusted friend.

"Speaking of the man of the hour, here he is."

Dakota winked at her, before he sat down for a moment at the table with to his brothers. Before long they were passing jokes back and forth to each other.

"I didn't realize Dakota had six brothers." CoraLee

leaned over to speak in Sarah's ear as the sound of laughter got louder.

"Yes. I think they've always been close to each other."

"Seems to me, that each of them were given an extra dose of good looks." CoraLee spoke softly as her gaze studied the brothers at the table next to them. "Take Hunter for instance. Even with that scar on his cheek, he is still a very appealing and handsome man."

"Oh, really?" Sarah leaned closer until she was eye to eye with her best friend. "Do tell. What is it about Hunter that appeals to you?"

"Stop teasing me. I just think he's handsome, but he's also very irritating and high-handed. He'd be a great husband for some weak-willed girl that doesn't have a mind of her own, but not for me."

"Hmmm. To quote Shakespeare, "Methinks the Lady doth protest too much." Sarah winked at her friend.

"Let's not talk about me." CoraLee's cheeks had turned a lovely shade of red from their conversation, which Sarah found very telling. "I'd rather hear about you. How's it going with you and Dakota?"

"As well as can be expected. This is just a marriage of convenience, after all." Sarah's fingers fiddled with the new wedding ring on her left hand.

"I think it's much more. Dakota's eyes are glued to you, Sarah. It's like you've just lit up his world. Sort of like the way he's looking at you right now."

Sarah turned her head slowly, to see Dakota's dark penetrating gaze latched onto her. Her heart beat faster, and the corners of her mouth lifted before she turned to talk to CoraLee.

"Well, it's all part of the deal we made to act like we're in love when we're with our families. So if you believe it, then our acting skills are better than I thought." Sarah shoved back any thoughts of attraction for her new husband.

"Yeah, sure. You keep believing that." CoraLee shot her a I-don't-believe-you look that she'd used ever since they were in grade school together. "But, just for the record, I think you two would make a great couple if you'd ever get over your hang-ups with each other."

"Well, I'm not convinced."

"Maybe your husband can convince you then, because he coming this way." CoraLee spoke in a half whisper, looking over Sarah's shoulder.

Sarah looked up just in time to find Dakota standing in front of her.

"May I have this dance, Mrs. Callahan?"

"Of course." Sarah placed a trembling hand into her husband's steady one.

They walked over to the dance floor that the musicians had set up for dancing.

Someone had added tiny lights to the trees that surrounded the green grass, leading to the cabin.

Dakota's hand on the small of her back was warm as he led her to the center of the dance area.

A singer crooned a love song in the background, while Dakota slid one hand to her waist and held her hand with the other.

Out of the corner her eye, Sarah could see many of the wedding guests watching them as they moved together in this first dance as husband and wife.

"Nervous about having these people with their eyes on us?" Dakota leaned forward and pressed warm lips against her forehead. "Don't worry, I've got you in case you fall."

"I appreciate that."

She peered up at him. Dark eyes met hers, and an electric jolt rocked Sarah, as though she touched a live wire. A breathless panic filled her, and she longed to pull her eyes away, anything to escape the fluttering sensation in the pit of her belly.

"Perhaps our families need to be convinced of our devotion to each other." Dakota's warm breath whispered in her ear.

Suddenly, he moved both hands around her waist and pulled her closer. Sarah put her hands lightly on his shoulders, but Dakota moved them higher to encircle his neck.

"Now, we're dancing like newlyweds." Dakota looked down at her, the mellow lights shining like a homing beacon in his dark eyes.

The feel of his arms around her brought with it a jumble of emotions. His touch felt warm and gentle, causing her pulse to trip over itself. When his gaze slid to her lips, desire shot through her, leaving her breathless.

She yearned for him to kiss her right there and then.

Dakota tilted her face up to receive his kiss. As his lips met hers, the pressure of his mouth was as light as the evening sun touching the ocean.

As her knees started to weaken from his lingering kiss, Sarah forced herself to pull her arms away from around his neck.

"I think we've convinced them." Sarah whispered as she stepped back a little.

Their kisses had begun to talk her heart into believing that maybe it would be possible for them to fall in love.

It scared her.

No, she couldn't allow herself to fall any deeper in love with Dakota.

She needed to guard her heart. She couldn't risk loving her new husband only to be rejected again.

CHAPTER SIX

akota

ABSENTLY, Dakota patted the top of his dog's head as he walked from the barn to his cabin.

He had been eager to check on his property after he had been away for a long time.

As far as he could tell, it looked like the barn, cabin and land had been kept in good order. Next time Dakota saw his brothers Hunter and Sawyer, he would need to thank them for faithfully checking up on his place while he'd been gone.

Seeing the smoke rising from the chimney, he thought of Sarah. The woman who was now his wife.

Sarah MacDonald — er, Sarah Callahan. He would have to get used to the fact that he was now a married man. Even though it was a fake marriage, he was committed to it at least until Sarah's grandfather agreed to move to town.

Limping up the steps to the front door of the cabin, he hesitated. Would he find Sarah awake?

It was so strange to come home and find someone else waiting for him. His dog wagged his tail impatiently beside him.

"I know, Sarge. I'm eager to warm up by the wood stove too." He turned the door knob quietly, not wanting to wake Sarah. "Well, there's no time like the present."

Opening the door, the scent of bacon hit him. Turning his head, he saw his new wife busy frying bacon in the skillet.

"Oh good, you're back home. The bacon is almost done." She turned and smiled wide at him. "How do you like your eggs cooked?"

Dakota stepped into the house and taking off his wet shoes, put them on the rug near the wood stove.

"Scrambled is good." Dakota was surprised to see her up so early and cooking breakfast. "Thanks."

He motioned for his dog. "Sarge. Sit. It's time to clean your feet."

Obedient as ever, his dog sat on his haunches with one paw held up so that Dakota could reach for it. Grabbing a clean cloth, he rubbed the mud from first one paw and then the next, until all four paws were cleaned.

Rubbing his furry head, Dakota whispered. "Good boy." He handed Sarge a treat, which his dog quickly ate before he went to lay down near the wood stove.

"Your dog listens so well." Sarah commented as she put

the bacon and eggs on two plates and set them on the small kitchen table.

"He does. Sarge was originally trained as a Police dog, so they learn to obey quickly. In the line of work I do, quick obedience can sometimes be the difference between life and death." Dakota quickly washed his hands at the sink and sat at the table beside Sarah.

"I can understand that. Maisie was not trained like that, but she listens well enough for a rescue dog." Sarah smiled as she studied Sarge.

"Yeah, she does. Are you glad you left your dog with your grandfather?" Dakota knew that Sarah loved animals.

Whether it was dogs, cats, cattle or horses. One of the things he really appreciated about her, was the way she cared for four footed creatures. A love for animals, was something they had in common.

"Yeah. Grandfather needed my dog, more than I did. She follows him outside and barks whenever she senses danger. I feel better knowing Maisie is there with him. However, I admit to missing my dog already." Sarah offered a wistful half-smile. "So, Sarge will no doubt get a lot of attention from me."

Dakota grinned. "He'll soak it up. Sarge lives for attention."

"Good." Sarah smiled wide at him, a sparkle in her green eyes.

Dakota sucked in his breath. He could hardly believe that he would have this beautiful woman living with him as his wife for the next few months. It was surreal.

Deep inside Dakota was certain he would enjoy her

company. He would just need to make sure he didn't allow himself to get used to it.

Finishing his meal, he sipped the last bit of coffee. Sarah stood to her feet and grabbing the coffee pot, poured more of the hot brew into his mug.

"Thanks." Dakota sipped more coffee. "Well, we should make plans on how we're going to search for Mindy." He grabbed a notepad and pen from off the small shelf that stood behind the table. "I think better on paper."

Sarah nodded. "I understand that. And yes, we need some kind of strategy. That precious little girl must be very scared."

"Yeah." I did have my assistant PI, Milo out here doing a search for her while I was laid up with my wound. But he didn't find any new clues." He shook his head, frustrated that he'd come up empty handed.

Sarah sipped her coffee, waiting as he wrote on the notepad.

"I was thinking for today, it might be good to stop by the Sheriff's office to see if they've learned anything new. Also, we should ask around at some of the more common places folks in town hang out."

"Like the diner, the coffee shop, the yarn place and any other place you can think of." Dakota was busy writing down the ideas as he was speaking them.

"And, we should consider taking a look at the playground. The one near the swimming pool and also the playground near the Elementary School." Sarah said. "That way we might have a better chance of spotting the little girl."

Dakota nodded. "Yeah. Let's do that." He was glad that

Sarah shared her ideas with him. They needed to work together to find little Mindy.

"What about Harry's Bar and Grill?"

"Good idea. We should stop by tonight. In the evening, is when most folks stop by to grab food and sit at the bar and enjoy some dancing. We could join them and see what we can find out from some of the locals." Dakota continued to jot things down.

"Folks that live here year round would likely notice someone that seemed unfamiliar." Sarah put a finger on her chin, deep in thought.

Dakota nodded and stood to his feet carrying the dishes to the sink. "Yeah, they would. Okay then, let's get going." He whistled for his dog.

"I'll put Sarge in the back yard. I built a fence and a large dog house a couple years ago, so with a little water and food he'll be fine until we get home."

Dakota hurried to the back door with his dog following closely at his heels.

Opening the door, Sarge followed him outside. He poured dog food and water into each dog bowl.

By the time he arrived back in the kitchen, Sarah was already waiting for him. She had changed into a dark green sweater that brought out the sparkle in her large green eyes. Her long strawberry blond hair was in a pony-tail and she looked amazing.

Dakota set a guard up against emotions that threatened to spring up and bubble over. He refused to let the guard down around his heart. In his mind, if he started to get sentimental about his fake wife, it would spell trouble for both of them.

Especially since they were in the middle of a mission to find a kidnapper.

So, instead he focused on the mission at hand. "Ready to go?"

Sarah nodded. "Yes."

Dakota was grateful the drive into town didn't take very long. He was far too distracted by his lovely wife.

Stopping the truck in front of the police station, they got out and walked into the building. "I just need a few minutes to talk to Sheriff Turnbull."

"Okay. Mind if I tag along?" Sarah's impish smile was hard to resist.

"Of course." As they stepped into the police station they spotted Sheriff Turnbull.

The Sheriff looked up from a conversation he just finished, and spotted him.

"Sheriff, if you have a few minutes to spare to talk about this missing persons' case, I'd be grateful." Dakota shook his hand.

"Yes I do. Follow me to my office, it's quieter there." Sheriff led the way and noticed Dakota limping from the wound. "How's the leg?"

"It's healing slowly but surely." Dakota winced rubbing his leg. "But, I married the woman who helped with my leg wound, so I suspect I'll heal much faster now."

Dakota winked and grinned at Sarah whose cheeks turned a pretty rose color.

"I heard about that. Congratulations to you both." Sheriff smiled and then turned toward Dakota. "I only have a few minutes before I'm needed elsewhere. You had questions?"

"Yeah. Just curious if you found any more clues about Mindy Bellanger or any leads on the identity of the kidnapper?" Dakota's expectant gaze focused on the Sheriff.

"Sorry, I don't have any new information for you. My deputy and a couple of my officers looked around and asked questions, but no one has seen a new little girl or the kidnapper who stole her away." The Sheriff rested his chin on his clasped hands for a minute.

Then an idea hit him. "I think you should have a chat with a retired Private Investigator. He's tracked and brought to justice all sorts of suspects and I think he would have some helpful advice." Sheriff wrote on the back of his police business card. "His name is Art Mulreedy and he lives on the northern edge of town. Here's his address."

Dakota took the card. "Looks like we still have some work to do, to find the missing little girl. However, we will get to the bottom of this and find answers. I appreciate your help. Thanks, Sheriff."

"Glad to help." Dakota and Sarah shook the Sheriff's hand. They started to walk out of his office when he spoke again, his face clouded with uneasiness. "One more thing. Sarah, your stepfather was released from jail a few weeks ago. I just thought you should know."

The color drained from Sarah's face and Dakota put a steadying hand around her shoulders. When she spoke, her voice was strained. "Thanks for letting me know Sheriff. Hopefully there won't be any reason for us to see each other."

"That's understandable. However, if he becomes a

problem let me know and I'll deal with him." Sheriff Turnbull's voice held a firm determination, that helped relieve her mind of worry.

"Thanks, Sheriff. We appreciate it." Dakota smiled and looked at Sarah and together they walked out the doors of the police building.

Sarah sighed heavily as they neared the truck, crossing her arms over her chest in a protective gesture. "I have to admit I'm scared now that my stepfather is out of jail."

Dakota put his hands on her shoulders and looked into her eyes. "I understand you're afraid of your stepfather. You have every right to be. But, I'm asking you to believe that I will do everything in my power to protect you. Do you believe me?"

Sarah swallowed and nodded quickly. "I believe you, Dakota. Thank you. I don't know what I'd do if I didn't have you to help me through this."

He leaned his forehead against hers. "Good thing you don't need to find out, because I am here for you."

She tilted her head up and he saw the tell-tale sign of moisture in her beautiful green eyes.

With his thumb, he gently wiped away a stray tear on her cheek. "Feeling better?"

Sarah nodded and smiled. "Yes. Much better, thanks."

Dakota was relieved.

Tears made him feel so helpless. Especially when they came from a woman he cared about.

Dropping his hands from her arms, he stepped back suddenly needing to do something so he wouldn't give into the need to pull her into his arms and kiss her senseless.

Clearing his throat, he spoke quickly. "I think I'll go have that chat with Mister Mulreedy. Do you want to come with me or would you rather stop by *A Goode Yarn?*"

"Hmm. I'll visit Lynda Goode's shop I think. That way we will be getting more done in the same amount of time. I can walk. It's just down the street." Sarah turned to him. "Meet you at the *Little Bean Cafe* in an hour?"

"Sounds good." Dakota watched her walk away, already missing her — which to his mind was a ridiculous notion.

Forcing himself back to the business at hand, he got in his truck and drove to the street address the Sheriff had written on the back of the card.

It was an old clapboard style home, with paint peeling off the outside walls like old wallpaper.

Carefully, he walked up the rickety wood steps that led to the front door. He knocked three times before the door opened.

"Mr. Art Mulreedy?"

"That's me. What do you want?" The man standing on the other side of the screen door wore a glower the size of Montana. The steely sound of frustration and annoyance edged his low voice.

Dakota hesitated for a moment, caught off guard by it. "Sheriff Turnbull gave me your name. He thought you might be able to offer me some advice." Dakota handed Mister Mulreedy his Private Investigator card with his name and other details.

"Well, if the Sheriff sent you here for advice, you must be in desperate need. Come on in." The older man opened the door wide, and Dakota stepped inside. "Follow me to the kitchen. I always find it easier to chat while sipping a hot cup of Joe. Dakota is it?"

Dakota nodded smiling and soon found himself seated at an old wood table.

Soon the coffee was percolating in the background and Mister Mulreedy sat down at the table.

"So is this about a case you're working on?"

"Yes, Mister Mulreedy it is."

"Please, call me Art. It's much easier." Art stood up and after pouring two mugs of coffee, he set one down by Dakota. "Here's cream and sugar if you like."

Placing the two items on the table, he sat down and sipped his coffee looking expectantly up at Dakota.

"Thanks, Art. To answer your question, yes, I wanted to talk to you about a case I'm on, involving a missing seven-year-old girl. The clues I found seemed to point to Refuge Mountain, but so far I haven't found anything concrete."

"Start from the beginning. Tell me details." Art listened intently as Dakota shared about the clues he found in the backyard of Mindy's parents' home in Colorado. He added that he hadn't found anything else to go on that would lead them closer to the kidnapper.

"Wait, did you say someone shot at you?"

"Yeah, but that was on the mountain. I don't remember seeing anyone around me at the time. Most likely, it was a stray bullet from someone who was around there, hunting deer." Dakota sipped his coffee. "Sheriff also had a couple of his officers search the area. The officers even questioned an old man who lives there, but they didn't find anything either."

Art pondered that, but didn't say much about it. "Maybe. All right, what about the matches you found?"

"Yes, they had the logo from our town pub, Harry's Bar and Grill. My wife Sarah and I plan to stop by tonight to ask around."

"Your wife? You are either foolish or brave to bring someone you love into this line of work with you, I haven't decided which." The former P.I. shook his head slowly. "Based off my own sufferings when in love, my answer would be that you have a little bit of both."

Taken aback at the sudden change of topic, Dakota didn't know what to say. He was thinking of a response, when Art Mulreedy focused back to their original subject of searching for the kidnapper.

"What about the other clue — you said something about boots?"

Dakota shook his head, trying to keep up with the man. It took him a moment to catch up with what the former P.I. was saying. "Right, the boot prints. I was hoping you would be able to help with that. I don't know if — in your years of experience — you have come across a brand of leather boots that leave a star shaped imprint on the ground?"

Art raised an eyebrow and nodded. "Hmm, that sounds familiar. I can't say for sure, but lucky for you I've saved all the documents of every case I ever worked on. But, you'll need to give me a day or two to see what I can dig up."

"Fair enough. I appreciate you doing that." Dakota stood to his feet. "Well, I should go. Thanks again for your help today, Art."

"Since, the Sheriff recommended you talk with me. I figured I should at least know the reason for it. On top of that, I don't like injustice in any form, but most especially when it involves children." The older man mumbled as he followed Dakota to the door. "Come back in two days. Hopefully, I will have found something useful by then."

"Sure thing. Thanks." Dakota hurried to his truck and drove away. The cantankerous and bitter old man had annoyed him. What was that random comment that Art made about him being foolish enough to involve someone he loved in his line of work?

It made him curious to know more about the former P.I.'s story. What happened to Art Mulreedy that caused suffering in his love life, how did he become such a grumpy, bitter man?

Dakota expelled a breath.

Parking in front of cafe, Dakota sat still for a moment. He thought of Sarah. While it was true that she was involved in helping him find the missing little girl, it wasn't like his heart was on the line.

Dakota walked into the cafe and searched for the woman who had filled his thoughts all day. He found his wife sitting at a corner table and looking out the window.

Staring at Sarah, Dakota's heart hammered against his ribs. A strange inner excitement filled his belly whenever she was near. An undeniable attraction was building between them and it bothered him.

These feelings weren't part of what he'd planned on in this marriage-of-convenience to Sarah.

They had an agreement. They had a fake marriage. They had decided not to fall in love.

It was settled.

Then why at every turn, did his heart betray decisions his rational mind had already made?

As he walked toward Sarah, he did his best to mask his inner turmoil with a deceptive calmness.

Clenching his jaw, a new determination set in. He decided to do whatever it took to force these new emotions under control.

⁂

SARAH LOOKED up and her heart lurched madly inside her chest at the sight of her husband.

He had always had the ability to stir her emotions ever since she was a teenager. Back then, he'd always seemed so far above her that she felt anything between them was hopeless.

Now, at least she would be his fake wife — even though it was an arrangement that would be short lived.

But, even seeing him across a crowded room, her fake husband could stir her emotions. There was this magnetic pull that drew her to him.

At this moment, Dakota's look of determination, caused an uneasiness to race through her.

What had happened to the calm and relatively happy man whom she had talked with only a short while ago?

"Hi." Sarah looked over at Dakota with a warm smile, hoping to coax him into a better mood. "Did you have a good talk with Mister Mulreedy?"

Dakota shrugged. "It was informative. I'll need to go back to see him again in a couple of days. There's some information from his cases as a former P.I. that he wants to share with me."

"That's helpful."

"Yeah. It is." Dakota nodded.

The waitress stopped by and took their small order for a minute, leaving soon after.

"And you? Did you learn anything new at the yarn shop?" Dakota took a sip from his water glass, his dark eyes studying her over the rim.

"Nothing really. Jean told me that they didn't see a lot of new children at the elementary school where she works, and when they did it was noticeable." Sarah shrugged. "Alice told me she hasn't seen anyone new at the homeless drop-in center or food pantry where she volunteers. So far, it feels like searching for a needle in a hay stack with little to no results."

The waitress returned with their specialty coffee orders.

Dakota stirred his coffee his focus clearly somewhere else.

A furrow formed between his brows. "Yeah. It seems like it will be difficult to find Mindy right now, but we can't give-up hope. That little girl's life might very well depend on us finding her."

"I know you're right. We will search until we find her. That's all there is to it." A new determination filled Sarah. A warmth filled her as she realized they were working together as a team to find Mindy.

An hour later Sarah was still appreciating the fact that her and Dakota were working as a team as they drove home.

Dakota checked on his dog while Sarah changed her clothes, opting to wear a soft pink blouse and a navy blue skirt that twirled as she walked.

Taking her hair out of the pony tail, she brushed it until it flowed smoothly down to her waist. Since their destination was Harry's Bar and Grill, Sarah decided a fun night was as good a time as any for a change.

Dakota parked the truck in front of the roadhouse pub. He walked her to the front doors and leaning down whispered. "You look beautiful tonight. I love it when you leave your hair hanging loose like that."

She turned to him, a warmth flooded her belly to see his gaze riveted on her. The dark eyes that stared at her were as soft as a caress.

She tried to throttle the dizzying current racing through her.

Heat rose up to her cheeks at his compliment and she whispered softly. "Thanks."

As they stepped inside the lounge area of the road-house pub, Dakota's hand rested on the small of her back.

A warm glow filled her and she couldn't help but feel protected by her husband. She had to fight the fact that her feelings for him were intensifying.

Country music played softly in the background and over that they could hear the loud chatter of people's voices.

"Let's go sit at the bar. We'll have a better chance of talk to folks there." Dakota slipped his arm around her waist and walked with her to the bar.

Sarah sat down on a tall stool, she looked around and recognized one of the bartenders. "Jerry Fletcher, it's been awhile since I've seen you. Grandfather is eager to have that re-match chess game with you."

A stocky man with a protruding belly and greying hair turned to her, with a grin. "Ah Sarah, it's been awhile since I've seen you or your grandfather. And yes, I've been meaning to call Angus to setup that re-match with him. Time just keeps getting away from me."

Sarah smiled. "Well, grandfather will be glad to hear from you."

"Good. I'll call him soon. Meanwhile, it's good to see you Sarah, and you Dakota. What can I get for you?" Jerry smiled at her as he dried the large glass cup in his hand.

"I'll have a soda." Sarah turned to look at Dakota beside her. "But, there was something else we were hoping you could help us with."

"Sure. What's up?" Jerry poured soda into a glass cup and added ice before handing it to her.

She turned to Dakota who pulled out a photo.

"We're looking for a little girl. Her name is Mindy, she's seven years old and was last seen by her parents in their backyard in Denver, Colorado a few weeks ago." Sarah explained. "Does this photo look familiar — have you seen this little girl anywhere around town?"

Sarah handed the picture over to Jerry. She had the picture of this little girl in her mind. She wore a pink t-shirt and had long wavy brown hair and brown eyes. Mindy looked similar to many little girls she had seen in the past few years.

Sarah had done her best to learn by heart Mindy's features so that hopefully she'd be able to see her when the time came.

But, memorizing details was never something she'd been good at. Even during her school years, she would learn something and forget what she learned the next day.

But, she was determined to try her best and not forget this time.

Jerry picked up the photo and looked closely for a minute. He shook his head as he gave the picture back to Dakota. "I'm sorry. I haven't seen her."

"Thanks for taking a look. Would you have any ideas about who might have seen her?" Sarah knew it was a long shot, but she asked anyway.

"Not off the top of my head, but if I think of someone I'll let you know." Jerry gave her a quick nod before hurrying to help the next customer.

Deep grooves formed between her brows as she turned to Dakota. "It looks like we'll need to keep asking around."

Sarah bit the bottom of her lip as worry for little Mindy surfaced.

Dakota grimaced and squeezed her hand softly. "Don't worry. We will find her no matter how many people we need to talk to."

"Okay." She swallowed, forcing a smile.

Images of children she would often babysit when she lived with her grandfather came to mind. Those children were so innocent, curious and kindhearted. Why would anyone want to hurt one of those little ones?

Memories from her own childhood with her abusive stepfather tried to force their way to the surface, but Sarah quickly pushed them down.

She didn't want to think about that right now.

An increasing sense of urgency flooded her senses. They needed to find Mindy — and soon.

Dakota looked around nodded at a few people he knew. "Let's go talk to a few more folks here."

He stood to his feet and Sarah slipped her hand in his. Dakota seemed to know quite a few folks who had come to Harry's Bar and Grill, because he stopped to talk to at least three different people.

However, no one recognized the child in the photo.

They walked further, until a friend of his recognized him.

"Dakota Callahan, you came back home." Sally Guthrie spoke to him from a booth seat near the window. Her and her husband were eating their meal. Sally changed places to sit beside her husband. "Come sit with Ted and I."

Dakota grinned and pulled Sarah with them and soon they were seated across from the married couple.

"And who is the lovely lady you have by your side, Dakota?" Sally pushed her glasses up on her nose and a wide smile on her lips.

"This is my wife, Sarah." Dakota turned to her, squeezing her hand.

Sarah couldn't deny the pleasure she felt at being introduced as Dakota's wife, even though it was truly not quite real.

"Oh my. I never thought I'd see the day. From our days in High School, I was convinced you were a die-hard bachelor, Dakota." Sally looked at Dakota and winked at Sarah.

"Well, I guess I hadn't counted on Sarah winning me over." Dakota turned to her, his rogue smile firmly in place, and Sarah could feel heat rising from her neck to her cheeks.

For a fleeting moment, Sarah felt herself believing his words along with the look in his, then just as quickly forced her confused emotions into order. She reminded herself, that he was just acting the part of the adoring husband.

She smiled back, hoping her expression held the same adoration. The only difference was that the loving look on her face, was very real.

"Well, I never thought I'd see the day." Sally whispered shaking her head. "I'm happy for you Dakota and Sarah, congratulations."

"Thanks." Dakota nodded.

"So what are you up to? Are you still working for the FBI?"

Sarah couldn't help but notice Sally's curiosity about her husband. She wondered if they used to date each other? A flicker of jealousy rose up in the inside, but she quickly tamped it down. She had no right to be jealous. After all, together they had agreed to a marriage-of-convenience.

Mentally, she chastised herself for allowing her emotions to get the better of her and forced a smile.

Dakota replied. "I retired from the FBI a couple of years ago and now I work as a Private Investigator."

"Oh, that sounds interesting. Any interesting new cases you're working on now?"

"Actually yes. I'm looking for a missing little girl right now. We've been asking around town if anyone recognizes the girl in the photo." Dakota pulled Mindy's picture from his pocket.

Sally looked closely at the picture and showed it to her husband Ted.

"Does she look familiar?"

Sally shook her head. "I love this little girl's red hair, but her features don't look familiar, I'm afraid. How about you, Ted?"

Ted shook his head. "No, I don't recognize her."

Dakota sighed heavily. "Well, thanks. Most folks around here have told us that. If you have any ideas of other places where we could look, let me know. That would be appreciated."

"Wait a minute." Sally turned to Ted. "Didn't the Heeter family just foster or adopt a little girl?"

Ted slowly nodded. "You might be right."

"There's an idea." Sally smiled. "Dakota you should pay a visit to Mel and Dorothy Heeter. I think they have nine or ten children and they just took on another little girl."

"Thanks for letting me know." Dakota quickly wrote down the family's address.

They talked a little longer with Sally and Ted until the couple left.

A live country band started playing a slow song, but Sarah continued to think about the little girl. Why did it seem as if little Mindy was nowhere to be found?

Dakota stood to his feet and leaned over whispering in her ear.

"You need cheering. Dance with me."

She slipped her hand in his and he pulled her close to him, leading her onto the dance floor.

As the lead singer crooned a slow western tune, Dakota pulled her into his arms.

"What's got you all worried?" Dakota's whispered words warmed her ear.

Sarah had a difficult time thinking coherent thoughts as she was held close in her husband's arms.

"I was just thinking about that lost little girl. I just can't believe it's taking so long to find her." Her voice cracked and she swallowed back emotion that threatened to spill over.

"You're really taking this hard, aren't you?" She could feel what felt like a kiss on the top of her head before he pulled her close. "Shh. It will be okay." Dakota had one hand on her waist and with the other he caressed the top of her head. "We will find her, I promise."

Sarah could feel his uneven breathing on her cheek, as he held her close. She relaxed, sinking into his cushioning embrace.

She fit so perfectly in the hollow between his shoulder and neck. For the first time she was able to mentally describe how being with Dakota felt like to her.

Being with him was like coming home.

A home where she was safe. A home where she mattered. A home where she was loved.

Even though she knew it couldn't last, she allowed herself this moment to enjoy feeling loved.

Sarah decided she would store this moment in her memory and hang onto hope that it would be enough to last her a lifetime.

akota

"Looks like the rest of the family is here already." Dakota parked his truck and came around to the other side to open the door for Sarah.

He looked at the large Callahan family gathered around Mack's gravesite. His mother had longed for a way the family could honor her husband's memory. She decided to have a memorial every year sometime in December.

The family already shared a lunch together, but his mother insisted on meeting at her husband's gravesite as well.

Dakota was always amazed at the deep love that was shared between his father and mother.

He always thought he would never find someone like

that. In fact, he'd been determined to never open his heart to love like that for fear of losing them.

Since holding Sarah in his arms last night at the road-house pub, he couldn't stop thinking about her. Dakota realized that his feelings for his wife were intensifying and he didn't really know what to do about it.

All night long, he'd tossed and turned and woke up from a lovely dream about Sarah.

Reason warned him to keep his distance, but it seemed his heart had a mind of its own.

He slipped his arm around Sarah's waist and let his hand rest there. They were supposed to act like they were a newly married couple in love. Problem was that for him, it was starting to not feel like an act anymore.

Sarah sent him a warm smile, leaning close to him as they walked towards his family.

"Dakota and Sarah, I'm glad you're here." His mother walked towards them, giving them each a warm hug.

"Of course we're here Mom. If it's important to you, then it's important to all your family." Dakota hugged his mom and kissed her cheek.

"Ah, Dakota. You're so like your father. You always seem to understand how to make me feel valued and loved." Annie Callahan's gave him a soft smile.

She turned to her sons, their wives and her grandchildren and spoke gently. "I'm so happy we could get together to celebrate your father today. Since, his favorite time of year was Christmas — it seems appropriate that we gather as a family as we near this special time of the year." She paused for a moment and looked around. "Well then, I thought perhaps we could each say something about your grandfather that you were thankful for. That would be a wonderful way to end this memorial in his honor."

Each of them walked closer to their Dad's headstone until they all stood in a semi-circle together as a family.

"Wyatt why don't you go first?" Annie Callahan looked towards her oldest son with an expectant smile.

Wyatt nodded and taking off his cowboy hat, he held it to his chest. "I have so many wonderful memories of Dad. He was a strong man who spoke his mind and who could muscle his way through whatever life dealt him."

"But he was also a faithful and loyal husband, father and friend. I will always be grateful for Dad and Mom for choosing me to be their son. I love and miss you, Dad." Wyatt looked at the gravestone and reaching for one of the roses his mom held in her arms, he laid it on the cold dirt in front of his father's gravestone.

Dakota stood by quietly listening and watching as the rest of his brothers and his sister-in-laws shared their tributes to his father.

His heart was full as memories spun around and around in his head.

When at last it was his turn to speak, it took him a full minute before he could say anything.

Swallowing back emotion, he began with a voice that was grave and raw. "Mack Callahan was the first real Dad I ever had in my life. When my biological father died suddenly when I was just a small child, it was just me and my mother and my sister."

"At the tender age of seven years old, both women I adored were taken from me also." Dakota stared at his father's gravestone as emotion welled up inside of him. He felt the warmth of Sarah's small hand as it slipped into his. He was grateful for the comfort her nearness brought him.

Sighing heavily, he continued. "Life had given me a lot of scars and wounds. And to top it off, I had a chip on my shoulder. The day Dad and Mom chose to add me to their family, I went with them reluctantly."

"However, as I became part of the Callahan family, Dad was patient with all the ways I tested and challenged him. He told me he loved the fact that half of my identity included American Lakota First Nations ancestry."

"I had been mocked and called names by other students in my early elementary school years because of my heritage. But, Dad taught me to appreciate and embrace every part of who I am."

"It's because of Dad's encouraging words that I had the courage to accept the warrior side of me and enter law enforcement. I will always be grateful to Mack Callahan for that. Dad, you will forever be loved and remembered."

Dakota picked up a long-stemmed rose and laid it on the dirt by his father's headstone.

His mother laid the last rose down on the dirt and with her gentle voice began to speak. "Mack, you've heard from your family this day. You were loved and appreciated in unique ways by each one of us. I am thankful for the many ways you loved me and believed in me during our over fifty years of married life. Thank you, my darling. I miss you and love you."

His mother turned to look at each of them, as tears flowed down her cheeks. "Thank you to each of you, for indulging me so we could honor your dad today. I appreciate you all."

"The tributes that each one of you have spoken about your father has filled my heart with so much love and joy. I've been reminded again what a wonderful family you are to me. I love each one of you."

As the memorial for their dad began to wind down, Dakota and Sarah had a chance to talk with everyone in the family.

Sarah joined Abby and Sierra to talk with them while his brother Hunter joined Dakota. "Thank you for sharing about your struggles with bullying and the unfair treatment you went through because of your heritage. I'm glad Dad was there to help you to embrace your true identity."

Dakota watched as Hunter clenched his jaw, tightened with strain. "Sometimes a person can go through difficult circumstances or situations as an adult that can leave them wrestling for years with their identity."

"I've experienced some of that since my injury a few years ago. I wish Dad could have been here today to give me some much needed advice." Hunter sighed heavily and looked down as he scuffed the toe of his cowboy boot against the ground.

Dakota put one hand one his brother's shoulder, sensing Hunter needed encouragement. "Hey man, it's okay to wrestle with who you really are, especially when circumstances come into your life that have changed how you see yourself."

"I think to some degree, that happens to everybody. Like Dad told me, the important thing is to embrace who you truly are. That's what I needed to do and I'm a better man because of it."

Hunter gave him a quick hug. "Thanks Dakota. That's a helpful reminder and just what I needed to hear today."

"I'm glad." Dakota watched as Hunter went to join the others.

Soon Sarah walked his way with his three nephews by her side.

"These boys had an idea they want to run by you." Sarah turned to Dakota's nephews a big smile on her face.

"Remember when you said we could do something fun together, Uncle Dakota?" Joey had sprouted so much in the past two years that his head now reached Dakota's chin.

"I do remember. What's your idea?" Dakota looked at each of his nephews, loving the fact that they wanted to hang out with him.

Joey grinned. "We were hoping you'd let us come with you to get the Christmas tree — Sarah said you might do that tomorrow."

"She did?" Dakota saw Sarah shrug and smile. "Well, as it turns out, that sounds like a good idea. We'll be sure to take Sarge with us and a sled to pull the tree home."

"Thanks, Uncle Dakota." All three boys seemed to speak at once.

Sarah grinned as the boys hurried away. "You're fairly popular with those nephews of yours."

He shrugged. "They'll do anything to spend time with my dog."

His wife leaned close and whispered. "I think they

would do anything to spend time with their favorite uncle too. I know, I would."

Dakota's pulse quickened at her words. He loved how her cheeks stained pink when she impulsively spoke what she was thinking.

Sarah had always been like that. She was more open and honest about her feelings than he ever had the courage to be.

He wanted to reach over and pull her into his arms and kiss her soundly, but they had an audience. Besides, what he really needed to do, was to bring his emotions under control.

With each passing day that he spent with Sarah, it was growing more difficult not to give into these growing feelings for his fake wife.

"I'll go double check about tomorrow with the boys' mothers." Sarah hurried towards where Abby and Sierra were talking with each other.

Seeing each family member in deep conversations, Dakota turned to take a short walk.

As he walked passed the gravestones in the cemetery. He thought about the people who had died and wondered what they had done with their lives. Did they like the lives they lived? Did they have families who missed them still?

Dakota was just pondering those questions, when he spotted a man about a hundred yards in front of him.

The large man wore a furry hat with a plaid winter jacket and warm gloves.

With one hand he held his hat against his chest as he stood over the gravesite.

As Dakota watched him, it almost looked like he was

saying a prayer. He must have really loved that person who passed away, for whom he paid his respects.

Snow started falling as the man stood there.

He looked so lonely and forlorn.

Suddenly, he reached inside his jacket and pulled out what looked like a teddy bear or a doll. Dakota wasn't sure what it was.

After the man set it down by the headstone, he put his hat back on his head and hurried away.

Curious, Dakota walked toward the gravesite where the man had been standing.

When he arrived at the gravesite, he looked down and saw it was a little girl's gravesite. This little girl had only lived eight years before she died. On the gravestone was written: *Hannah Sophia McCoy beloved daughter.*

Dakota's gaze drifted down until he spotted an old-style doll dressed in raggedy clothes. The doll had long dark brown hair and big brown eyes.

It was a little girl's doll the man placed near the grave. He must have loved her very much. Was the child his daughter or a sister?

As Dakota stared at the doll, an odd nagging at the back of his mind refused to be stilled. There was something familiar about this doll that he couldn't quite put his finger on.

Without thinking, he reached for the doll. Holding it in one hand, he snapped photos, hoping that at some point the reasons the doll seemed familiar would reveal themselves.

All of a sudden, the loud sound of his phone rang out in the stillness of the afternoon air.

Setting the child's doll back down by the gravestone, Dakota answered his phone.

"Hi Cameron. What's up?" His assistant spoke came through on the other end of the phone line.

"I've been researching the backgrounds of those involved in this kidnapping case. I've discovered some new details that you may not like."

Hearing Cameron's warning, Dakota's ears perked up. "I'm ready. Tell me what I need to know."

"To start with, Sarah's stepfather is related to our missing girl." Dakota began walking back and stopped when he heard that piece of news.

"What? Okay, you'll need to explain how that's possible."

Cameron began. "Well, Mindy's Dad— Chase Bellanger — his father is Henry Bellanger. Henry was a wealthy business owner. However, not many folks know that Henry had a brother whose name was Thomas. Henry and Thomas's father Herbert Ballanger, disowned Thomas, when he was only twenty-three years old."

"And the reason the father had for disowning Thomas?"

"I couldn't discover the specific reason why Herbert disowned his own son." Cameron continued in calm, soothing tones. "But, when he did, Thomas left and basically got a new identity. He went by the name Tom Bellans."

"Tom found a job as a miner and got married. They had two daughters and a son — Saul Bellans. Life wasn't good for Saul and his sisters because their father — Tom

Bellans — would often come home drunk and would physically abuse his wife and children."

Dakota sucked in a breath. "So basically, Saul Bellans had a terrible childhood and ended up repeating his father's mistakes."

"Yeah, that about sums it up. Sad isn't it?"

"Yeah." Dakota was deep in thought. Just how would this affect Sarah or Mindy for that matter?

"Thanks for doing all the research on this case, Cameron. This has been really eye-opening. I'll need to ponder this as well as let Sarah know more details about her stepfather."

"Of course, Dakota. Let me know if you need anything else." Cameron hung up the phone.

Dakota was stunned by the unexpected news about Sarah's stepfather.

Now that he was aware of this new information, it raised more questions than answers. He was determined to get to the bottom of it and find the answers he needed.

Knots formed in his belly as he walked towards where Sarah stood with his family.

How was he supposed to tell her more bad news about her stepfather? Would she have the strength to weather this new storm?

"RELAX. I'll make us some hot chocolate and then we'll talk." Dakota's solemn expression had remained solidly in place ever since they left the cemetery and arrived home.

Sarah shifted restlessly on the sofa, her slender fingers

fidgeting on her lap. With each minute that passed, she became increasingly uneasy with each one of her husband's measured looks.

"Here you go." Dakota handed her the steaming mug of hot chocolate, before sitting down beside her.

She lifted the mug closer to her nose and breathed in the scent. "Thank you Dakota. I can smell the cinnamon spice you added. Reminds me of Christmas. My grandmother used to bring me hot chocolate just like this. Thank you." Memories floated across her mind and she gave him a warm smile.

"You're welcome." Dakota took a sip of the hot drink, before setting his mug on the coffee table. "I told you we needed to talk and we do."

An uneasy feeling crept over her, and she suddenly sensed that she might need all her strength for this talk.

"All right. So, tell me what's going on?" Sarah chewed on her lower lip and stole a look at him.

With a quick nod, Dakota began. "My assistant uncovered more details about your stepfather."

Awkwardly, she cleared her throat even though her misgivings were increasing by the minute. "Go on."

Dakota went on to explain that he'd asked his assistant to research the backgrounds of all the people he had on a list.

"And my stepfather was one of them." At his nod, she forced a casual tone and asked. "So, what did you discover?"

"Well, my assistant found out that your stepfather is related to our missing little girl, Mindy Bellanger."

"What? How is that possible?" A shiver of anxiety

caused her hand to shake. She set the mug of hot chocolate down on the coffee table.

Dakota explained how Herbert Ballanger had disowned his son Thomas and had left everything to his son Henry Bellanger.

"But, my stepfather's name is Saul Bellans. How could he be related to Mindy Bellanger?"

"Well, it turns out after Thomas Bellanger was disowned by his father, he moved away and changed his name to Tom Bellans. He became a miner, got married and had two daughters and one son — Saul Bellans." Dakota sighed heavily.

"So, what you're really saying is that it's possible that my stepfather kidnapped Mindy Bellanger?" Icy fear twisted around her heart. Her stomach clenched tight as she thought of the scared and lost little girl.

"Yes, I'm afraid it's possible. With this new information, we now know he could have been motivated by a desire for more money or for revenge. Perhaps both." Dakota words sent a chill up her spine.

Wasn't it enough that her stepfather had physically abused her — did he need to also kidnap and potentially abuse another innocent child?

She felt as if a hand had closed around her throat. She swallowed in an effort to lose the constriction around her voice.

"Sarah, I'm sorry to have to tell you that." There was a tenderness in his gaze that was her undoing. "Are you okay?"

She nodded quickly and blinked back tears that threatened to spill over. "I'll be okay. I'm surprised and maybe a little overwhelmed. I just realized all the pain from the past regarding my stepfather isn't over after all. It's only just begun."

"First we need to find proof that your stepfather was involved. Just because he had a motive, doesn't mean he's the kidnapper. However, I promise to do all I can to discover the truth." He searched her eyes and slowly reached for her hands, rubbing his thumb gently over her smooth skin.

She nodded. Despite the fear that coursed through her veins from his news about her stepfather, she believed him. Dakota was a man of honor who wouldn't stop searching until he found out the truth.

"We'll make it through this together, Sarah." Warm tingles spread from her belly outward as her husband said her name.

Sarah squeezed the large hands that held hers. The nearness of him gave her comfort and she had to fight her overwhelming need to be close to him.

"Thank you. I feel better knowing that you're here. " She sighed. Her thoughts about her stepfather, aroused old fears. "I can't help but worry about little Mindy. I'm convinced we need to do everything possible to find her."

She shuddered as memories that haunted her for years came back in full force.

"I remember, how terrifying it feels to be trapped, alone and very afraid. That's how I felt for so many years." A hot tear rolled down one cheek as memories that haunted her came back to the forefront of her mind.

"It was right after my mama died, that things changed

and began to get worse. I had just turned six years of age and was grieving deeply the loss of my mama."

She swallowed back the emotion and continued. "I had just started School. My stepfather asked the neighbor, Mrs. Ellison to take care of me after school until he got home from working at the mine."

"When stepfather got home, he was usually half-way drunk because he already stopped at the pub to drink with his friends. He would tell me I was worthless, useless and that I should never have been born."

"Between the ages of six and ten years of age, there were many days when my stepfather verbally and physically abused me. The last time he beat me so badly that my one eye was swollen shut and my arm was broken." Sarah bit her lip hard to stop the tears from flowing.

"That was when Mrs. Ellison took me to the hospital and the police arrested my stepfather. That was the day my grandfather came to take me to live with him and grandmother."

A swift shadow of anger swept across Dakota's face as she finished telling her story. "That man should've stayed in jail with all the hurt and pain he caused you."

Sarah looked over at him, inwardly pleased that he would stand up for her and to protect her.

"Thanks for that." Her brows furrowed together in worry. "Now that my stepfather is out of jail, I'm worried. What if he is responsible for kidnapping that innocent child? I desperately want Mindy to be safe."

"I remember how terrifying it feels to be trapped, alone and very afraid. That's probably what she is feeling right now. We need to do whatever it takes to find her and bring her back home."

Her face clouded with uneasiness and anxiousness.

"Come here." Dakota wrapped an arm around her shoulder, pulling her close to his side. "Thank you for being so honest with me about your childhood. I'm so sorry you went through that cruel abuse as a young girl. No child should be made to suffer like that." He kissed the top of her head softly.

"I'm grateful you are here with me safe and sound. I'm also grateful that you are helping me to search for little Mindy. I'm completely committed to finding her. And we will find her... soon."

As he held her close, her heart turned over in response. He was so disturbing to her in every way and she couldn't help but feel like her love for him intensified the more time she spent getting to know him.

Learning of his passion for justice and truth and his compassion for little children were character traits that pulled her towards him.

As her thoughts drifted towards that lost innocent girl, she couldn't help but hope that she would be found soon.

Sarah also hoped and prayed anyone trying to harm little Mindy would be exposed and brought to justice soon... *even if the kidnapper turned out to be her stepfather.*

CHAPTER EIGHT

"You should listen to the doctor, grandfather." Sarah encouraged him, hoping he would try to be patient.

"Aye. But I am tired of the waiting for my leg to be fully healed. I think Mrs. Moore will see to it that I obey the doctor's instructions." Sarah heard a muffled voice speaking in the background and then her grandfather chuckled.

It was good that he had a good relationship with the nurse Dakota hired to help take care of him. "Before you go, I wanted to ask you something. Do you remember my friend Dermot — a stocky looking mountain man with red hair who has played chess with me a few times?"

"Of course. I remember all your friends, grandfather." Memories came back to Sarah, of the red haired man who stopped by a few times especially in the winter months to talk with grandfather and play a game of chess.

"Well, he stopped by the other day and mentioned how good you've always been with children. He has a niece visiting him from out East, but he needs someone to look after her, day after tomorrow. He wanted me to ask if you would be willing to watch her for the afternoon?"

Through the years, Grandfather had many friends who would ask her to watch their children.

She looked out the kitchen window and saw Dakota and his three nephews waiting for her. Distracted, she replied. "Sure, I can help out, grandfather."

"Good. I'll let him know. Since you'll be here, I'll tell Mrs. Moore she can take the afternoon off. I look forward to seeing you again, Sarah." There was a wistful sound in her grandfather's voice, and it warmed her heart to know he missed her.

"I miss you too, grandfather. And I look forward to spending time with you." Sarah smiled. "But for today, Dakota and his three nephews are waiting for me, so I need to go. We are picking out a Christmas tree."

"Sounds like fun. Love you, Sarah."

"Love you too, grandfather." Sarah clicked the off button on her phone and slipped on her jacket, hat and gloves and winter boots.

As she walked outside, the sound of boy's laughter greeted her. The snowfall that had begun last night, continued to fall onto the ground making the yard look like a fluffy white cloud.

She loved the freshness of new snow.

The boys were busy pelting snowballs at their Uncle and Sarge was barking and joining in the fun.

Suddenly, Dakota turned her way and called out. "Hey, look who decided to join us." At his teasing, his three nephews plowed her down with fistfuls of snowballs.

Laughing, Sarah made her own snowballs and flung them back at Cody, Tony and Joey. Soon all three boys were busy chasing Dakota's dog with snowballs.

Dakota walked towards her, his rogue grin firmly in place. He rolled a snowball from one hand to the other, like a juggler.

"Are you going to throw that big snowball at me?"

Dakota shook his head, but continued to walk towards her.

"Why not? What are you planning to do?" She threw two snowballs at him, each one hitting him in the chest. But her actions failed to stop him from advancing towards her.

Giggling, she turned on her heel and ran in the other direction, but she wasn't fast enough. All too soon he caught up with her.

Grabbing her around the waist, he swung her close and before she knew what he intended, he slipped the snowball down the back of her shirt.

"Eeek!" Sarah backed away from him, trying to escape. Losing her balance, she fell on top of the deep fresh snow, in an ungraceful plop.

She shivered from the cold, grimacing as she stared at him.

Dakota peered at her intently, seemingly checking if she was hurt.

"I'm cold and it's your fault." Her teeth chattered as she flung the accusation towards him.

"Well, that's what happens when you fling snow at your good-natured husband." Dakota teased and came over to stand next to her, his smile wide. "But to show you that I am a gentleman, I'll help you up."

He held out his hand.

She hesitated, not completely trusting the look in his eyes. "I don't think so. You might have another snowball in your hand just waiting for me."

Dakota placed a hand on his heart.

"I don't have a snowball, I promise. I wouldn't do that to you twice in one day." He murmured, his expression stilled and grew serious. Bending at the knees he reached for her.

With strong arms, he lifted her up and pulled her into his arms then stood to his feet.

Gently, he brushed the hair away from her forehead. His eyes darkened as his gaze met hers, drifting down to her lips and back up. He hesitated for a moment, as if waiting for her to object.

She was too surprised to do anything except cling to him. He leaned down and softly pressed his lips to hers.

He moved his mouth over hers, in a slow drugging kiss that left her breathless.

For Sarah, it seemed as if her husband had branded her, resealing their vow, making her his forever.

Shivers of delight followed his passionate kisses and she felt transported on a soft and wispy cloud.

Her emotions whirled and her thoughts spun around and around.

Dakota's kisses had a jarring effect on her senses, making her more aware of him than ever.

Sarah felt as if he had touched the deepest part of her being. Ever since she was eighteen she'd dreamed of being kissed by Dakota.

In less than a month, she'd been kissed twice by him. Happiness swept over her so impossibly deep that for a moment it trapped the air inside her lungs.

Dakota had taken her heart and touched the deepest part of her spirit and made her truly his.

She wanted desperately to tell him she loved him and she would, soon.

He pulled his lips from hers and stepped away, his every breath seen in the swirls as the warmth mixed with the cool air.

"Are you all right?" Dakota's voice was thick with concern.

Sarah blinked, nodding and a soft smile trembled over her lips.

"Good. I'm sorry, I shouldn't have done that." He ran a hand through his hair.

A remote look shadowed his face.

She knew that expression for what it was.

Regret.

Dakota was sorry he allowed himself to get close to her.

The bubble of happiness that had surrounded Sarah, suddenly popped. Dakota regretted holding her in his arms and kissing her.

The same moment that had been so intensely beautiful for her, had felt like a mistake to him.

It felt like her heart sunk to her toes at his apology. She swallowed back emotion that threatened to spill over messily.

She was still trying to figure out how to reply to him, when Dakota's dog jumped up against her leg.

She'd read somewhere that dogs had an instinct about the emotions of people. Maybe Dakota's dog knew she needed a hug.

Sarah threw her arms around him. "Thank you for the hug, Sarge. I needed that."

Dakota watched her for a moment, a brooding look on his face. "We should probably go get that tree. Then we can get back in time to bring the boys to town later."

"Yeah." They walked to where Dakota's nephews played together in the snow.

Sarah looked at each of them, very aware that all of them playing and having fun together felt very much like a family.

This was how she had always pictured a loving family would be. Her mom had died when she was far too small to remember much about her and her biological dad had died when she was only a baby. So the only glimpse she had of a loving family, was when she lived with her grandfather and grandmother.

That feeling of love, kindness and care for one another that she'd experienced with her grandparents, she craved that with a family of her own.

If Sarah were honest with herself, the true longing of her heart was that her fake marriage to Dakota, would become real.

That together they would be that loving family she'd dreamed about for so many years.

She felt a warmth flow through her at the thought.

As her thoughts drifted back to last night when her husband held her in his arms, she still felt cocooned in a warm glow of happiness.

Dakota's nearness and his kisses made her senses spin.

But, she needed to try to stop thinking about him, because it was obvious that he regretted their kiss.

"Ready to find that Christmas tree?" The man who filled her thoughts, interrupted her suddenly.

Heat stole its way upward, filling her cheeks. Her breath quickened and she hoped he couldn't tell what she was thinking.

Hurrying to catch up with Dakota, she attempted to ease any awkwardness between them with her usual method… with nervous chatter. "I'm ready. What type of tree are we looking for anyways?"

The boys were walking ahead of them into the trees. The afternoon sun shone bright even through the heavy trees.

Dakota pulled a long wooden sled behind him along with a chainsaw so they could cut down the tree quickly and get it home.

He called out to Joey. "Let's ask the boys. Joey, what type of tree should we look for?"

"A pine tree with lots of needles. And it's got to have that Christmas tree smell to it." Joey laughed. He was the one who came up with the idea of finding a Christmas tree.

Sarah chuckled. "Sounds about right."

Dakota grinned. "A pine tree it is. We'll see what we can find deeper in the woods."

They walked in the snow for another half a mile before Joey looked upwards and suddenly stopped. He pointed towards a tall pine tree. "There it is. That is the perfect Christmas tree. What do you think of that one, Uncle Dakota?"

"Looks good." Dakota turned to her with one eyebrow raised. "What do you think?"

Sarah looked up at the tree. She could see the branches looked a little lopsided on one side, but that didn't matter. If Joey and the others thought it was perfect, so did she.

She nodded. "I like it."

"All right then. Let's bring it on down." It didn't take long before Dakota had sawed through the tree trunk and the tree fell on the snow. The three boys lifted the large tree onto the sled.

"We can take turns pulling the sled." Joey handed the sled's rope to his brother Tony.

They trudged through the snow until a couple hours later, they finally reached the cabin.

They set up the tree inside the cabin in front of the large picture window. The Christmas tree filled the area, adding a brightness to the space that lifted Sarah's spirits.

Dakota nodded quickly. "Good, that's done. It's time to drive you three boys to town. We'll have lunch and your parents will pick you up from there."

All three of his nephews hurried to get their things ready.

Dakota's gaze met hers.

"I need to change into dry jeans. I'll be back soon." She nodded and hurried to her room. As she brushed out her hair, she expelled a long quivering sigh. Why did she have to fall in love with Dakota Callahan? Why couldn't she have fallen for someone safe and predictable like her friend Jerry?

Yet, for some reason it was Dakota who made her pulse leap with excitement. It was Dakota who made her heart sing for joy. It was Dakota who filled her dreams.

Yet, he regretted kissing her and holding her in his arms. Maybe he felt some affection for her, but as far as she could tell his feelings didn't go deeper. It was time she realized that Dakota would never ask her to be his real wife.

Feeling troubled and confused, she finished brushing out her hair and slipped on her favorite light pink sweater to cheer her.

When she stepped out of her room to join the others, she forced a smile. It was painful to be near the man she loved, knowing he didn't share her feelings.

A lump of suffocating pain lodged somewhere near her heart.

Sarah didn't know how she would make it to the end of this fake marriage with the pain that filled her heart. But, she must try.

THE MEMORY of Sarah's soft lips against his, seemed imprinted permanently in Dakota's mind.

As he drove the truck toward his appointment with former P.I. Art Moody, he remembered the subdued look on his wife's face even as they enjoyed lunch together in town.

She was so beautiful to him in every way, yet he'd hurt her. He was responsible for the strained look on her lovely face.

Dakota wondered if he had hurt his wife's feelings when he distanced himself from her.

Without a doubt, he enjoyed holding her in his arms and tasting her strawberry flavored lips. He could have gone on kissing her forever.

But he couldn't do that.

At the beginning of this convenient marriage, Dakota had resolved to guard his heart. He couldn't allow himself to get close to her --- to grow to love her — only to have her hurt or worse.

With the type of career he had, there was bound to be a suspect on the run who would do everything in his power to escape arrest — including harming or killing someone he loved.

Hadn't he already experienced the loss of his beloved sister and mother?

No, it couldn't be helped, he decided. He needed to hold on tightly to his resolve to keep his distance from his beautiful wife.

Knocking on the front door to Art Moody's house, Dakota girded himself with a renewed determination to guard his heart from the same woman to whom his wayward heart was falling for.

Suddenly, the door opened. The former P.I. stood on the other side of the screen door his stare drilling into Dakota for a moment before he spoke.

"Dakota Callahan. Just in time for a cup of Joe. Come in." Art Mulreedy's voice held a note of annoyance at being interrupted.

Dakota grimaced, wishing for a moment he didn't need the information that the former P.I. had to give him.

But, it couldn't be helped. He was desperate to catch the kidnapper and find the little girl and bring her home to her family.

The older man handed him the mug of coffee and sat across from Dakota at the kitchen table.

"How's it going with the case? Any progress in your search to find the perpetrator?" Mr. Mulreedy's dark eyes sought his.

"Not yet. So far, I've only discovered details that I'm not sure lead anywhere." Dakota sipped the coffee as he thought about the case. His gaze drifted to the small stack of papers on the table between them. "Were you able to find documents on the leather boots with a star imprint in the soles?"

The former P.I. grinned and nodded. "It's your lucky day."

Dakota sighed in relief. "Well, that's good to hear. What did you find?"

"I managed to dig up information on the type of boots you described." He pulled out a couple of pages that were filled with information. "What I found was, these boots were made especially for miners from the *Clear Springs*

Leather Company. However, this business closed for business about three years ago around the same time the mine closed down."

The former P.I. handed him the document where the information was listed in black and white.

Dakota grabbed it and nodded as he read through it. As he studied the information, he thought of what he needed. "So, this boot company closed down. I wonder if I can somehow get in touch with the former owner or manager of the company. I need a list of names of folks who ordered boots in the past ten years or so."

"Again, you're in luck." The older man's low voice carried a hint of boastfulness. "As it happens, I had a similar thought, realizing that you would need names of former customers."

Mr. Mulreedy pulled out a few more pages. "I talked with the former owner, and he gave me a list of customers from the last twenty years they were in business — specifically from folks who bought the boots with the star imprint in the sole."

"That's very helpful. Thanks. I'll need to narrow the list of names down to folks who lived and worked here in Refuge Mountain." Dakota took the documents that the older man handed to him and laid them in a row on the table, so he could see the information clearly.

"I thought I'd help with that too. If I'm correct, from the information we've been given, I've narrowed it down to five men who could be possible suspects. I've circled their names in red." The former P.I. pointed to three of the pages where there were names circled in a red pen.

Dakota raised one eyebrow and smiled. "This is really helpful. Let's see what who we're looking at."

He looked closer at the names of the men and read them out loud. "Corwin Thames, Leeland Allenby, Saul Ballens, Dermot McCoy and Fergus Drummond."

"Yep. Those are the names." Art Mulreedy finished drinking his mug of coffee, setting it down with a thump on the table. "It looks like now you're set. You just need to discover who matches the rest of the information you have for the kidnapper."

Dakota nodded and sighed. "Yeah. Not an easy task as there might be a few variables I haven't considered, but I'll figure it out. Thanks a lot for the extra research you did on finding where the boots were made and the customers who bought them, Art. I really appreciate it." Holding the papers in his hand he asked. "Can I keep these documents for a few days?"

Art Mulreedy nodded. "Yeah sure. Just get 'em back to me in one piece. I like to keep all the cases I've worked on in one place."

Dakota stood to his feet and shook the older man's hand. "Thanks again."

"It was a job that needed doing. Glad I could help."

Dakota walked to the door, but turned his head as memories invaded his thoughts.

"I remember from our last conversation, you told me I was either brave or foolish to bring someone I loved into this line of work. You then said based on your own sufferings in love, you believed it was a little bit of both."

The former P.I. nodded.

"Do you mind if I ask why?" Dakota felt a need to understand more about this man.

The older man paused for a long time, rubbing the bristles on his chin with one hand before answering. "I do mind, but I'll answer anyway. Perhaps, my answer might be helpful to you at some point."

Art Mulreedy's grave voice began. "Here's my story. I was twenty-six years old and had just got my Private Investigator's license. I was dating Wanda Beatty and had just asked her to marry me, when I had a high profile case offered to me where I would be paid handsomely. I accepted the case and worked around the clock trying to solve the case and catch the suspect."

He sighed and continued. "Wanda kept asking me when we should set the date for the wedding, and I kept putting her off. During the process of the investigation, I learned that the suspect had not only killed the company owner, but had also gone after his wife too, harming her and the children."

"I found myself paralyzed when I thought of a suspect in any of my cases doing that to anyone I loved. I told Wanda, we should postpone the wedding for a few months, telling her I was far too busy to marry at that time."

There was a bitter edge to Art's voice as he retold the story. "Wanda said she loved me and was willing to wait. When the time came that the case was solved, of course I started investigating another case. I asked Wanda if we could wait until the next year... out of fear."

He shook his head. "That's when Wanda told me, she was done waiting. That if I really loved her, I would marry her right then and let tomorrow's worries take care of themselves. I refused to back down and she gave me back my ring. The next year, I heard that she married another man — a police officer."

Regret and bitterness blazed in the faraway look in his eyes. "I was too fearful of what might happen to Wanda, if I married her. Then suddenly, she was gone. I wanted to protect her, but she ended up marrying a man whose job was not safe anyways."

"Looking back, I can tell you I did well in my career, but ended up alone. At the time, I thought I was doing the right thing and I'm glad Wanda wasn't hurt. But, sometimes I look back and wonder if things could have ended differently than they did."

"And yet, you say I'm both foolish and brave for wanting to protect my wife?" Dakota asked, feeling like he was missing something.

The older man explained. "You are brave to protect your wife, that's a noble thing. But, as you continue to do your job as a P.I. — if you believe that shielding your heart from those you love will make them safe — then I'm afraid you are mistaken and foolish. I learned, to my regret, that when I tried to shield the woman I loved, I only ended up losing her. Now, every day I live with regret and loneliness."

Dakota nodded, digesting the older man's words. "Thanks for being vulnerable and sharing your story. I will think on what you've said."

As he drove away, Dakota couldn't get the old man's story out of his head. The former P.I. let fear make the decision on whether or not to marry the woman he loved.

Now, he lived a life filled with loneliness, bitterness and regret.

He had always asked himself the tough questions.

Did he want to end up like Art Mulreedy when he was an old man?

If he didn't want his life to look like that, it might mean he had some changes to make.

CHAPTER NINE

arah

Sarah watched for a moment as Dakota's truck disappeared down the street.

Her mind still burned with the memory of his sweet kisses from the day before.

When he held her in his arms, she felt safe. She felt loved.

Being in her husband's embrace had touched the deepest part of her heart, making her truly his.

Yet, he had apologized. He seemed to regret kissing her.

In fact, he seemed to want to distance himself from her.

Last night Dakota had spent the entire evening

working in his office, while she spent the evening by herself. The only company she had was a book and his dog.

Today, they were continuing their search for the missing girl. However, since Dakota needed to talk to the Sheriff, she took the opportunity to have coffee with her friend.

Nonstop, the questions hammered at her. *Why did it seem like Dakota was distancing himself from her? Had she done something wrong or offended him in some way?*

Troubled, she walked to the end of the street and turning the corner saw the mechanic shop. McMaster's Garage was an automobile mechanic shop owned by CoraLee's parents, George and Mary McMaster.

Seeing her friend through the window, she waved and hurried inside.

CoraLee spoke up from where she worked behind the front counter. "I'll be done in a minute, Sarah. I've just got to get the information for this work order entered into the computer."

"Take your time." Sarah walked around the large waiting room, looking at the pictures of antique cars that CoraLee's dad had fixed up over the years.

It was a hobby of his. But now he had in his collection at least seven antique cars — many from the early nineteen hundred and twenty's or thirty's — that had been fixed up to look good as new.

Sarah was still admiring the posters, when her friend came up beside her.

"Ready to go?" CoraLee grinned.

Nodding, Sarah followed her friend out the door.

"Let's go grab some ice cream."

"Sounds great." Sarah chuckled at her friend's love of ice cream. All throughout their years in School together, CoraLee had always found an excuse to bring her to Brown's Ice Cream Shop.

After ordering their cones, they found a table in the corner by the window.

"It's been too long since I enjoyed one of these." There was a wide smile on her friend's face every time she licked the chocolate dipped ice cream cone.

"I'm sure. You practically starve yourself when you are on a modeling assignment." Sarah sighed as she looked at CoraLee's trim figure. "Even now, you are too thin."

CoraLee shrugged her shoulders. "Well, that's why I allow myself these little treats. I can eat what I want when I'm at home. However, when I return to Paris after Christmas, that's when I'll need to watch my diet very closely again. I've got to fit into those designer clothes they want me to wear for each photoshoot."

"You my friend, are so beautiful and live such a glamorous life. If I wasn't such a homebody, I'm sure I'd be jealous." Sarah smiled, studying her friend.

CoraLee had always been lovely. Her ivory skin glowed on a perfectly oval face that was framed by thick wavy reddish brown hair. Her pretty Grecian nose, large hazel colored eyes and generous lips combined to make a charming picture.

Her friend grabbed her hand and squeezed it. "You see? That's why I like you so much. You are so honest and have a very compassionate heart. For the record, I'm glad you're not jealous of me. You don't need to be — not ever — because you're beautiful just as you are."

"Ah, you always know how to make me feel better, CoraLee." Sarah leaned back in her chair, relaxed and comfortable with her long-time friend. "It's nice that you managed to come home for a few weeks anyways. Do you like working in your Dad's mechanic shop?"

CoraLee shrugged. "I don't mind. I like the fact that I'm helping my dad and my two brothers most of the day. With family you help where you're needed."

"That's true. But, that's only if they let you." A heaviness centered in her chest as she thought of her Grandfather. "My grandfather still won't move away from his place on the mountain. However, Dakota generously hired a nurse to take care of him, especially while his leg is healing. I'm very grateful for that."

Sarah sighed and her face clouded with uneasiness.

"I hope your grandfather changes his mind for your sake, Sarah. I know how you worry about him."

She nodded. "I do. But, he sounded chipper when we talked earlier."

"Good. And how are things going between you and your beloved husband?" CoraLee rested her chin on her hand, a bemused smile on her lips.

A melancholy frown flitted across Sarah's features.

"Uh Oh. From your expression, I'd say things aren't going well?" Her friend grabbed her hand. "Tell me. What's wrong?"

Sarah blinked back tears that wanted to fall. Without warning, a tumult of emotions she'd kept bottled up inside came tumbling from her lips.

She told her friend how Dakota had kissed her and then seemed to regret it immediately. "He told me he was sorry."

A quivering sigh accompanied the telling of what happened between them. "If I'm being honest, he's already touched my heart in so many ways."

"Meaning, you've fallen in love with your husband."

Sarah nodded as her eyes grew misty and wistful. "Fake husband. But yes, I have fallen in love with him. But, it won't do me any good. Dakota continues to distance himself from me."

She toyed with the spoon that lay on the table. "Maybe it's all for the best. This marriage isn't supposed to be real, anyway."

Sarah drew in a deep breath and forbade herself to tremble.

CoraLee grimaced. "Hey, I understand you're frustrated. But I really believe Dakota's actions show that he is deeper into this relationship with you, than you realize."

"What? Why would you say that?" She stared at her friend wide-eyed, startled by the suggestion.

"Well, the fact that you two had fun in the snow together and then he couldn't resist holding you close and kissing you, speaks volumes." An expression of satisfaction showed in CoraLee's eyes.

"I don't understand."

"Well, the fact that he couldn't wait to kiss you, speaks of his attraction to you. I think he loves being close to you." Her friend continued with quiet assurance.

"But, Dakota regretted kissing you afterwards, because he's afraid of his own feelings. I think your husband is terrified that he might be falling in love with you and feels like he needs to create some distance between the two of you."

A self-satisfied smile rested on her friend's lips.

Sarah shook her head in disbelief. "That's ridiculous. Dakota is a man that speaks his mind. Why wouldn't he just talk to me about how he feels?"

Her friend squeezed her hand. "Because to him love is one of the most fearful emotions he's ever had to deal with. Because this time, his heart is on the line."

Sarah let those words sink deep into her heart.

She wanted to believe there was hope for her relationship with Dakota, but struggled with uncertainty.

"Maybe that's true. I just don't know anymore, Cora-Lee." She struggled with doubt that Dakota's feelings for her would ever change from affection to love.

Her friend squeezed her hand. "Just give it time my friend. You might be surprised."

Sarah didn't think so. Dakota was kind and very generous to her, giving her everything but himself.

But, his heart was the one part of him she wanted most.

DAKOTA DROVE down the dirt road near the edge of town.

Sarah sat on the passenger side of the truck, fidgeting with her fingers and biting her lips.

He had always meant to protect Sarah from helping with this part of the investigation. He could feel it in his gut, that the search for the missing girl, was about to heat up.

"Would you like me to bring you back to the ranch?" Dakota stopped the truck on the side of the road, near their destination. He turned to her. "I would be happy to drive you home. You really don't need to do this."

His wife turned to him, a wobbly smile on her lovely face. As she spoke her voice wavered. "No, I don't want to go home. I refuse to allow past fears haunt me for the rest of my life." Releasing a long sigh, she continued. "I'll be fine."

He shot her a doubtful look.

"Truly, I will be okay. Besides you'll be there to protect me. So, what could he possibly do to hurt me?" There was a pensive shimmer in the shadow of her green eyes as she spoke.

He knew she was being brave and he admired her for it.

"Okay then. We'll get a little closer to the house to see if we can get an idea of what's going on." Dakota drove the truck a little further until they were only a short distance from the house.

He looked over at Sarah and saw her hands trembling. Reaching over he held her hand calming her. "It's going to be okay. We are doing this together, remember?"

"Yes, thanks for the reminder." Sarah released a shaky breath. "I think I'm nervous just seeing the old house again. It brings back terrible memories." She shivered and swallowed as she stared at the corner of the house which was visible. "That's why I've avoided going near this area."

He squeezed her hand again, his mouth tight and grim as he pondered her words.

Dakota was about to say something else, when he spotted movement. "It looks like your stepfather is leaving. He's getting into his car."

He watched as Saul Ballens backed his rusty car out of the drive and started driving down the road.

"That's our cue." Dakota started the truck and started to follow. Sarah's stepfather drove down a few backroads until he finally turned into an acreage with a small cabin surrounded by trees.

Dakota parked behind some trees so that they wouldn't be spotted following him.

"I wonder what my stepfather is up to?" Sarah's wide-eyed gaze followed Saul's movements from the car and into the cabin.

"I think maybe we need to check it out and see what's going on. It's possible our missing girl is in there." He opened the door to get out of the truck, when Saul hurried out of the cabin, got back in his car and drove away.

"Let's go see what's going on in that cabin." Dakota drove the truck onto the yard, curious what Sarah's stepfather was up to.

He grabbed Sarah's hand and put his finger to his lips to indicate silence as they walked up the steps to the front door.

Turning the door knob, he grabbed his concealed weapon and pushed open the door.

With a quick look to the left and right, he didn't see anybody lurking in the shadows of the small room.

Sarah followed as he walked into the cabin. There were only four rooms and he quickly looked in all of them, not finding anyone.

"There's no one here." He turned to Sarah.

Sarah opened up one of the boxes. "There's only pieces of wood in here."

Dakota opened up another box. "Yep. It's stacks of wood pieces and other products related to woodworking."

He stared at Sarah, baffled. "I have no idea what the wood is for, but I guess we can safely say our missing girl isn't here."

Sarah sighed heavily. "Maybe we need to go to my stepfather's house and talk to him."

He raised one eyebrow, surprised that the suggestion came from her. She had been so worried about seeing her stepfather earlier.

"You're sure?"

"Yeah. I need to see him one last time. Besides I would like to see if he has something my mother gave me." Pain still flickered in Sarah's eyes whenever she remembered the wounds from her childhood.

Her hand trembled as she closed up the lids on the boxes.

He didn't know what to say to comfort her.

So, he reached out and caught her hands with his. "It will be okay, Sarah. We'll do this together. I promise to do everything I can to protect you."

Her large green eyes took on a new brightness at his words. Her voice sounded raw and hoarse when she spoke. "Thank you Dakota. That means the world to me."

She swallowed and squeezed his hands, with a tremulous smile.

Pushing her shoulders back, she drew a deep breath and said firmly. "Let's go."

With a quick nod, he followed Sarah outside. Her determination was evident in the way she held herself straight as an arrow.

Dakota could admit, he rather liked the courage he saw in his wife as she prepared to meet her stepfather.

His brows drew downward in a frown.

What would they find when they got there?

DESPITE DAKOTA'S ASSURANCES, Sarah could feel her legs and arms shaking as they knocked on the door to her stepfather's home.

The only reason Saul continued to live in this house was because the deed was in his sister's name.

Looking around, sudden and swift memories came back.

As a little girl, she remembered her mama planting flowers in the front of the house, near the steps.

Sometimes she would bend down to help plant a new flower. They would do it together and then mama would laugh and pull her close in a deep embrace.

There was something so peaceful about being in the garden with mama. Being inside the house when her stepfather was home was unfriendly, had always made her want to run and hide.

Sarah was so deep in thought, that she didn't hear the door open.

"So, you came to pay me a visit, did you?" Her stepfather had a cold-eyed smile on his gaunt face. His hair was so thin, he was almost bald and his skin looked sallow.

Sarah stood there stunned at the sight of him. He looked so much older and almost sickly. So different than how she remembered him as a child.

Saul repeated in the same cool tone. "Well, what are you here for?"

Sarah swallowed convulsively and willed her hands to stop shaking. "I wanted to stop by to get some of my mother's things that she left for me."

For a moment her stepfather studied her intently, before looking at Dakota.

"And who's the guy you have with you?"

"Dakota Callahan." Dakota's firm voice interrupted. "I'm Sarah's husband."

"Somehow, you managed to find a man who would marry you. Will wonders never cease." Saul Bellans words were worn thin and hollow even as he mocked her.

"Well, get to it then. Anything of your mother's is still in your old bedroom."

Opening up the door, he waved them inside.

Sarah stepped inside, noticing the house was as cluttered and dirty as ever.

Looking behind her uneasily, she spoke to Dakota. "My room is this way."

She opened the door, and was greeted by a musty and stale scent to her room. Nothing had changed in it, from the time she went to the hospital and left her stepfather for good.

Suddenly, the memory of that night came back in full force. Her stepfather had drunk more beers than usual and bellowed at her when she burned the supper meal.

You can't do anything right. You are always wrecking things and costing me money. You are a stupid, stupid girl.

That was when he'd taken his belt off and begun hitting her. She had put her arms around her head to protect her head.

Then her stepfather must not have thought the belt was doing its job, because next thing she knew he had hit her arm with the beer bottle.

She cried out at the same time she heard her arm crack. In pain, she ran out the front door of the house. That was when their neighbor, saw her crying with her face bruised and her arm broken.

Their neighbor had rushed her to the Hospital.

Sarah shuddered as she remembered, that was the last time she saw or spoke to her stepfather.

"Sarah? Are you all right?" Dakota's low voice, interrupted her memories and she jerked back.

"I'll be okay. Just so many memories in this house. Only a few of them were good ones — the memories that included my mama." Hastily, he wiped away a stray tear that escaped.

"I'm sorry that you lived through so much ill treatment as a child, Sarah. It makes me want to give him a taste of his own medicine." Dakota replied in reckless anger, his dark eyes blazing with amber fire.

Softly, she put a hand on his arm. "I know the feeling of anger, because I've spent many years being knotted up inside with it." Sarah shook her head and sighed heavily.

"But, it's not worth it to lash out at my stepfather. We will feel better if we've decided to take the high road and not lash out at him. Besides, I can tell he lives with a mental anguish of his own making. He's an angry, lonely and bitter old man who most likely looks back at his life with regret. Our anger won't change anything, so I think it's best if we just let him be."

Sarah looked over at Dakota with earnest eyes, hoping he understood.

He nodded and sighed, resting his large hand over hers. "I suppose you're right. But, I'm only holding back because you asked me to."

"I know, Dakota. And I do really love that you want to protect me. But, this time I really think we should just let it go."

"All right." He squeezed her hand, with a faraway look in his dark eyes. "You remind me of my mother. She was always a peacemaker and very wise. I always admired that."

Sarah was surprised at his admission. "Thanks. It means a lot to me to hear you say that."

For him to see her in as favorable a light as his mother, was high praise indeed.

"Welcome." Dakota removed his hand from hers and looked around the room. He seemed disturbed by their intimate conversation. "What do you want to take home?"

Sarah bit her lip and looked around the room, remembering why she was here.

She just wanted to retrieve a couple of things that

mattered to her the most. There wasn't any point to continue crying over what she had lost.

Walking over to the closet, she opened it to find her small jewelry box still there.

Opening the lid, she picked up the silver bracelet with the attached silver key.

Happy memories surfaced as she thought of when mama was still alive.

The bracelet had been a gift from her mother for her birthday. She remembered mama's words when she opened the gift. *It's a special bracelet Sarah, just for you. It's silver with a key attached to it. The silver sparkles and I know how you love sparkly things. This silver key has a special meaning. If you look at it closely, you see it's like a mirror. That reflection of you is the secret to open any door that's locked. Remember that. You are courageous, smart and full of love. I love you, granddaughter.*

A warm glow flowed through Sara as memories washed over her. She turned to Dakota who was watching her intently.

"My mom gave me this. This bracelet and mama's old jewelry box is what I want to take home with me." She looked around the bedroom. "There's nothing else I need from here."

Dakota nodded. "Well, let's get going then."

Sarah led the way down the hall toward the small den. She stopped when she saw her stepfather sitting in his old recliner, drinking beer and watching T.V.

He turned to them and spoke gruffly. "You can see yourselves out."

"We will. Thanks stepfather." Sarah stepped forward about to leave, when Dakota put a hand on her arm.

"Just a minute. I have a couple of questions to ask Saul first." Dakota spoke with a firm tone of voice.

"What is it?" Saul sounded irritated at the interruption.

"I'm searching for a little girl who went missing a couple of weeks ago. Her name is Mindy Ballenger. Does that name sound familiar?" Dakota boldly met her stepfather's eyes as he waited for an answer.

"The name does ring a bell. My father was a Ballenger, but he changed his name to Ballens before he had us kids." Saul shrugged.

"Have you met Mindy Ballenger or her parents Chase and Amanda Ballenger?" Dakota kept firing questions his way.

Saul sighed. "No I haven't. I just got out of prison. Being in the slammer didn't give me much of a chance to meet people."

Sarah grew restless at the exchange and looked at Dakota, trying to hint that they should leave.

But Dakota, had a few more questions.

"Can you remember where you were on November ninth?" Dakota was focused on getting answers.

"If you must know, the doctor forced me to stay in the Hospital from November seventh to the eleventh so he could prod and poke me with needles." Saul Bellans voice grew irritated. "So if you believe I took that little girl, think again. I can barely move around nowadays with all this cancer in my body — so how would I manage to carry off a little girl?"

Dakota pondered that for a moment, before he nodded quickly.

"If that's all the questions you have for me?" Saul's mouth spread into a bleak tight-lipped smile.

"Yeah, that's all. Thanks." Dakota nodded at Saul and turned to Sarah. "Let's get going."

Sarah hesitated and looked at her stepdad. "There is something I need to say to you stepfather."

Her voice was shaky, but she needed to get this said between them.

"Yeah what is it girl? I don't have all day." Saul turned to her, his unfriendly face making it even more difficult to say what was on her mind.

"I wanted to tell you, you really hurt me years ago with your hurtful words and your physical abuse. It's taken me a long time to heal.

Saul shifted in his chair, but no words passed through his lips.

"You might not want to hear this, but I need to say it anyway.

My grandmother — who passed away a few years ago — requested something of me, that I wasn't sure I would ever have the strength to do."

Sarah swallowed back emotions and continued. "My grandmother said: *I'm asking you to forgive your stepfather. Not because he needs it... but because you need to forgive him. Do this, so a root of bitterness doesn't grow inside of you and swallow up all the happiness in your life.*"

"So, right here today, I'm honoring her request. I've decided to forgive you stepfather. In spite of how you have wronged me, I choose forgiveness. The truth is, I might need to keep forgiving you as the years go by and as different memories return. But, today I choose to forgive you. I hope there comes a day when you choose forgiveness too, stepfather."

Sarah trembled and turned tear filled eyes to Dakota. She was comforted by the gentle look in his dark eyes and by the hand on the small of her back.

Turning back to her stepfather, she could see he was already watching his TV show and drinking the next beer bottle. He'd turned up the volume on the TV.

Sarah sighed heavily. And turning to Dakota said. "I guess that's our cue to go."

Hurrying out of the house, they got inside the truck.

Sarah turned to Dakota she murmured. "That was a difficult thing to do, to forgive him. But, my words didn't seem to affect him at all."

Dakota reached over and held her hand. "Maybe there's no softness in him anymore. I've heard that can happen to folks."

She nodded. "The other surprise was when I learned that my stepfather is dying. I didn't realize that."

"Well, in spite of that, he's still a mean old man." Dakota grimaced as he started the engine. "But, it's good to know that he didn't kidnap Mindy Ballenger. He really does look too sick to pull something like that off. I'll double check the Hospital records just to be sure."

She nodded. "Yeah. But, there's a small part of me that can't help but feel sorry for him. He's lonely, bitter, angry and now he's dying."

Dakota shook his head, eyeing her with a look of faint amusement. "You have a soft heart, even if it's misplaced in this instance. Even still, I believe I've come to appreciate that side of you."

There was a spark of some indefinable emotion in her husband's dark eyes as they held hers.

Her heart turned over in response. For a moment it looked like he wanted to say more, but the line around his lips tightened and he started driving.

"Thanks for that." Sarah appreciated the compliment, but wished he had said more of what was on his mind. But, in all the time she'd known him, Dakota had always been a man of few words.

When he was ready, he would share more about what he was thinking and feeling.

Sarah just hoped, she wouldn't have to wait too long.

CHAPTER TEN

 akota

DAKOTA WOKE up to the scent of cinnamon buns.

Looking at his watch he saw it was still early in the morning.

Peering out the window the sunrise was just starting to make its way over the mountains behind his house.

Snow fell softly to the ground, turning his land sparkling white. It was a clean and fresh look that had always reminded him of the fresh hope that surrounded this time of year.

He could hear Christmas carols playing in the background and a lilting voice humming along.

Why was Sarah up so early in the morning?

After slipping on a pair of jeans and pulling on a t-shirt, he walked towards the kitchen and stopped suddenly, when he saw his wife.

Her strawberry blond hair was tied back into a pony tail and she had an apron tied around her waist that hung loosely over her skirt. His wife looked like a mother from one of those golden days T.V. shows.

A sudden longing hit him.

He wanted this.

A place to belong. A family of his own. A wife who loved him.

He looked out the kitchen window and saw the snow falling gently to the ground. Wasn't this the time of year to believe in the impossible?

Hope. Miracles. Love.

Wasn't that the reason why his Dad had always loved this time of year? He had always been told that Christmas was supposed to be a time of hope, miracles and love. Hope for a better day. Miracles for the impossible. Someone who loved you for who you are.

As he watched Sarah, he was aware that he felt all three of those qualities whenever she was nearby.

Watching her yesterday with her stepfather had only increased the respect he had for her. When he wanted to take his anger out on Saul Bellans, Sarah had asked him to let it be. To choose to be a peacemaker instead.

It was very difficult for him to not want to physically hurt the man who had hurt Sarah. He'd grown up winning battles with his fists and he was ready to do it again.

Yet, because Sarah had asked him instead to let it go, he did.

He couldn't help but admire his wife for making that

difficult choice. To his way of thinking it would have been easier for Sarah to get angry at the man who had made her life miserable as a child. Instead she chose to do the opposite. She chose peace.

She was so disturbing to him in every way. Ever since they started this fake marriage, his feelings for her had deepened. She was growing on him, and he was powerless to resist.

Her presence gave him joy. The world seemed cleaner and brighter somehow, whenever she was near.

Dakota leaned a shoulder against the wall as he studied her. "Smells like Christmas in here."

She turned in surprised to see him there.

He turned up his smile a notch.

Sarah wiped her hands on her apron, her whole face spreading into a smile. "I thought with the snow falling outside and the tree in the living room, it seemed like the perfect day for Christmas baking."

Dakota's dog groaned from where he lay near the kitchen table. "Even my dog has been lured by the promise of delicious food."

Sarah giggled. "I don't think he's too interested in cinnamon buns, but perhaps I could give him a treat?"

"Yeah. Not too much though, or he'll get out of shape. I need him in shape to help me catch the bad guys. Right, Sarge?" The dog thumped his tail when he heard Dakota's voice.

Sarah gave the dog a treat and patted his head. "You're a good boy. Thanks for keeping me company."

"I don't think it was too difficult for my dog to keep you company. You've pretty much got Sarge wrapped around your little finger." Dakota felt irresistibly drawn towards Sarah. He walked towards her and cupping her chin, he searched her eyes before he offered a throaty whisper. "I know the feeling."

As he heard his wife's sharp intake of breath, his smile turned up a notch. His gaze drifted to her cheeks which had turned an adorable shade of pink.

"You have evidence of all your hard work on your face." With his thumb, he gently wiped away the flour that was scattered across one cheek.

"Thanks." Sarah looked so adorable as she stared at him, her large green eyes serenely compelling.

He slipped his arms around her waist and started to lower his head to kiss her beautiful pink lips, when suddenly his phone rang.

She withdrew from his arms, looking flustered.

Reluctantly, he pulled his phone from his pocket. "I should get this." He left the kitchen briefly to talk to the caller.

When he returned, his wife was busy washing dishes.

Dakota relayed to her the details. "That was the Hospital. They confirmed that your stepfather was in the hospital during the days that Mindy was kidnapped. So, I think we can safely take him off our list of suspects."

Sarah nodded. "I'm not surprised. When we saw him yesterday, he looked too sick to do much of anything." She sighed heavily. "So, what do we do next?"

He rubbed the back of his neck, moving restlessly. "I have to get back to work and dig deeper into the backgrounds of the list of suspects. I need to figure it out quickly."

"Yes, we need to find the kidnapper quickly. Every day that passes us by, is one more day that innocent little girl is at the mercy of the person who took her." Sarah replied in a low tormented voice.

"We will find him, Sarah."

She nodded. "I just wish I could stay here and help you. I am expected at grandfather's cabin soon. I'm to babysit a niece of one of his friends, Dermot McCoy. It was a last minute thing, but I told him I would help out."

Dakota nodded, distracted by thoughts of the case. He needed to double down on reviewing the facts of the case and do more digging into the background checks on not only suspects but those people close to them.

"There has to be an answer somewhere." Dakota murmured. He started pacing along the kitchen floor.

Sarah slipped into her jacket, putting a scarf around her neck.

"Well, don't wear a hole in the floor with all your thinking." She smiled and impulsively kissed him on the cheek. "I need to get going. Don't wait up for me. Hopefully, I won't be too late getting home."

"All right. See you later." He waved at Sarah as she left the house and walked to his office, determined to get to the bottom of who kidnapped Mindy Ballenger.

"HELLO, SARAH." Grandfather limped over to her with crutches under each arm. She hung up her jacket on coat rack and frowned.

"Hi grandfather." Sarah's gaze studied him. "You

shouldn't be standing. You're supposed to be sitting down with your leg propped up."

Grandfather shook his head, giving her a crooked grin. "Now, you're starting to sound like Mrs. Moore."

Maisie hurried into the room, at the sound of Sarah's voice. She bent down to hug her dog's furry body. "Have you missed me?"

Her dog's tail wagged and Sarah gave her one more hug, scratching her behind the ears before standing to her feet.

"I just saw Mrs. Moore driving away as I got here. How is it going with your new cook anyway?" Sarah always felt a need to know details when it came to her grandfather. For all the years she'd known him, he had never been very forthcoming about what was going on, unless she pressed him for answers.

"Good." He shrugged and turned to limp back into the living room. Sitting down in his favorite chair, he lifted his wounded leg onto the ottoman.

"But…" Sarah helped get her grandfather settled comfortably in his chair.

Grandfather sighed. "Aye, you know me well. But, Mrs. Moore is always forcing me to eat all the healthy food she cooks. I don't have any fun anymore, not like I had when you were doing the cooking."

Sarah chuckled. "You know very well, I cooked what you wanted me to most of the time."

She shook her head smiling. "For the record, I think it's wonderful that Mrs. Moore is cooking all this healthy food for you. You'll live longer that way."

Grandfather shook his head, a wry glint in his eyes. "I thought you'd see it that way."

Hearing a bumping noise, Sarah turned her head. Standing in the doorway of her old bedroom she saw a little girl with short red hair poke her head around the corner.

"Sarah, meet Lilly." Grandfather looked from Sarah to the little girl.

Sarah, saw Lilly and walked over to her. Seeing the little girl's wide-eyed look, Sarah crouched down to try to put her at ease.

Her big brown eyes and the short bob style in which she wore her red hair, looked cute on her.

"Hi Lilly, I'm Sarah. I hope we can be friends." Sarah whispered with a smile on her face, hoping it wouldn't take long to turn the uncertainty in Lilly's blue eyes, into a look of trust.

Lilly merely nodded. She didn't say anything, but simply stood motionless staring at her, clinging to the little doll she held under one arm.

As Sarah looked at Lilly's doll, an odd twinge of familiarity hit her. There was something about this doll with its long dark brown hair and brown eyes that Sarah felt she should remember from somewhere. Yet, the details slipped from her memory.

The doctor told her because of the trauma Sarah had endured as a child she might have trouble remembering details in certain situations.

Sarah was frustrated at herself for failing to recall details. But, she quickly tamped down those feelings.

Maybe something would come back to her later. Right now she needed to focus on Lilly.

"Should we do something fun together?"

The little girl nodded.

Sarah asked. "What should we do?

Lilly held out the dolly in her hand.

"Play dolls? That's a good idea. I'll go find the doll I have in my bedroom and we can play together." Sarah walked into her bedroom and opening her closet, she found her favorite doll from when she was a little girl.

Lilly was waiting for her, when she turned around.

Sarah showed the little girl her doll and explained. "My grandmother made this doll for me when I was only a little older than you are now. Grandmother said she made it to help remind me of my mama."

"You see my mother died when I was only a very little girl. But this doll, has always made me happy because her dress is made from the same cloth as my mama's favorite blue dress."

Lilly touched the doll's blue dress that Sarah held in her hands. As one tear ran down her cheek, the little girl slowly spoke. "Mama."

Sarah's heart was touched and she asked. "Do you miss your Mama?"

Lilly nodded, holding her doll close to her chest.

"My grandfather said your uncle brought you to his house for a visit. Since, your mom and dad had an emergency, they asked your uncle to take care of you for a few weeks."

"I understand that you live in the east somewhere. Do

you remember the name of the town?" Sarah hoped to get to know the girl better. She hoped perhaps if Lilly talked a little about herself, she wouldn't be so afraid.

Lilly nodded but continued to stay silent. She began to run her hand gently down the dresses on both dolls, to try to smooth out the wrinkles.

"They both look beautiful." Sarah saw that the little girl was determined to do what she could to take out any imperfections in the doll's clothes.

Sarah thought she'd try again to get to know her better. "Is your home near the ocean?"

Lilly shook her head. "Mmm… mountain."

Puzzled, Sarah tried to think of places in the East that had nearby mountains.

"My doll's dress is wet."

"Oh? Did your doll accidentally fall in the snow?" Sarah touched the doll's clothes and it felt really wet to the touch.

"Uncle said I lost my doll, but he found her outside."

"Well, I'm glad you have her back now."

The little girl took their dolls and brought them to the homemade dollhouse to play with them. Sarah followed along, still hoping that they could be friends.

They did things together for the rest of the afternoon. Sarah made spaghetti with meat sauce for their supper, but Lilly wasn't saying much more.

After supper, her grandfather told her. "Dermot should be back soon. He was buying another load of supplies to bring to his cabin. He likes to get enough food and supplies to last at least three months, so he doesn't need to go to town so often. He's become a real hermit ever since his wife and daughter died a few years ago."

Sarah had always wondered why he was such a loner. "Well, maybe having his niece for a visit will be good for him."

"Aye, maybe it will at that." Grandfather eyed the little girl who was starting to play with the dolls again. "I think Lilly has taken to you. You've always been so good with children. It will be good when you have some bairns of your own to love."

Sarah could feel heat rising to her cheeks at grandfather's suggestion that her and Dakota have children. "We don't want to rush anything, grandfather."

Her grandfather grunted. "It's no rush. It's time." Smiling, he walked back to his favorite chair by the fireplace.

Knowing the topic of children, was one they wouldn't agree on, Sarah chose to let it go. Instead, she went back to playing dolls with Lilly.

"We could make this home like your own home. Did you say it was near the mountains?" Sarah asked, hoping Lilly would open up and begin talking to her.

"Denver." Lilly whispered, using her shirt to clean off nonexistent spots on her doll's face. She seemed determined to get rid of all the flaws from her doll. "Mama and me and my dad live in Colorado."

Maisie walked into the room and rubbed her furry body against Lilly." The small child hugged the dog, who licked her face. It seemed she found comfort and love from the friendly pet.

Stuttering she whispered. "I miss my family and my dog, Charlie."

Sarah was puzzled by this new information. Colorado, was in the west not the east. Why did her uncle explain that she was from the east?

She couldn't figure out the answer, but something seemed strange. "I noticed that your doll looks similar to you. The only difference is your doll has long brown hair and you have short red hair."

"Mama got her for my birthday." Tears trembled on her eyelids as she smoothed her doll's dress again.

"That's a wonderful gift. It's like having your own twin." Sarah smiled.

As they continued to talk, Maisie walked over to her spot in the corner of the room and was soon fast asleep.

Sarah continued to play dolls with Lilly until she began to get restless.

"Let's see if there are some cookies in the kitchen." Sarah reached out and Lilly grabbed her hand.

Sarah searched through some of the containers on the kitchen counter, before she found the one with chocolate chip cookies.

She gave a cookie to Lilly and had one herself. They had just finished eating, when suddenly Sarah heard knock at the door.

"I think your uncle has arrived. He's ready to take you back home." Sarah stood to her feet.

Lilly stood too, but her legs and arms were shaking. "Not my home. I don't want to go back."

Sarah was questioning Lilly's comment, when the innocent child placed her little hand in hers. Together they walked toward the front door.

Dermot McCoy stood there, with his hands his belted

jeans, and his plaid shirt sticking out from the curve of his belly.

"How's my little niece doing?" Dermot low tones, seemed to scare Lilly as she crept closer to Sarah.

The little girl stood mute, without speaking to her uncle.

As she helped Lilly get her coat on, Sarah suddenly had a stark realization.

She turned to Dermot McCoy. "Lilly said she's not from the East but from the West. Her family lives near the mountains in Denver, Colorado. Why are you telling everyone she's from the east?"

Dermot's gray eyes glittered and his cheeks started turning red. "So, my little girl has been talking out of turn has she?"

He turned to Lilly, the tone of his words sharp and unkind. "That's not nice Lilly, especially when your uncle was kind enough to find your wet doll outside and bring her back to you. Why do you speak to Sarah, but not to me?"

Lilly looked up wide-eyed and began to tremble.

Sarah pulled the little girl to her side trying to calm the quivering of her little body.

"Lilly told me she doesn't want to go back to your cabin tonight." Sarah had a sudden thought. "Why don't you let her stay here with me and grandfather? We'll take good care of her and we'll bring her back to you tomorrow."

Dermot's expression clouded with anger and he replied sharply. "No, I'm afraid I can't do that. My niece needs to come with me tonight."

He moved to take Lilly with him, but the little girl still clung tightly to Sarah. "My brother and his wife have trusted me with her safety while she stays with me and I mean to do just that."

Sarah tried one more time to get the mountain man to change his mind.

"I really think she wants to stay with me. It would be fine with grandfather and with me to have her here." Sarah tried to talk some sense into the rugged mountain man, but he shook his head.

He was having none of it.

As her gaze met his, Sarah thought she glimpsed the shadow of fear glittering in his eyes. What was that about?

Suddenly his tone of voice switched from one of anger to a tone that was as smooth as silk. "On second thought, I think it would be better if Lilly stays with you."

Sarah sighed in relief. "Good. I think you made a great…"

Dermot interrupted. "Which is why I must insist you come with Lilly and me."

She sputtered, bristling with indignation and anger. "I can't go with you. My grandfather and my husband will worry."

The mountain man stepped closer, his expression clouded in anger. Pulling out a gun from under his jacket, he whispered in a low growl. "You see what I have here?"

Sarah nodded and her stomach clenched tight in fear.

"Good. Now do as I say. Don't scream or get wise and yell at your grandfather either. He's sleeping peacefully on his recliner and we don't need to disturb him. I was hoping to avoid this, but now you've gone and asked too many questions. So, I must insist that you come with us."

Dermot pushed the steel edge of the gun against her back.

"One more thing. Pull your phone out of your pocket. You can leave that behind." Dermot had stopped suddenly, waiting for her.

She fumbled her hand in her the pocket of her jeans and pulled her phone out placing it on the counter top. She had turned the volume way down on her phone when she got to grandfather's cabin.

What if Dakota tried to call her? Maybe, her grandfather would hear the phone and answer.

"Good. Now let's go." Dermot McCoy once again forced the gun against her ribs.

Icy fear twisted around her heart.

She was afraid for Lilly's life. She wouldn't be able to live with herself if she was the reason that innocent little girl was hurt. In order to protect Lilly, she had no choice but to go with Dermot McCoy and Lilly to his mountain cabin.

Sarah walked out the door, holding tightly to the small girl's hand.

They had just made it down the steps, when Dermot grabbed her arm roughly and forced her to walk in front of him. The steel end of the gun pressed against her back as he hurried them towards his truck.

Sarah shivered with fear.

Once again, her safety was in the hands of a wicked man. Only this time, it wasn't from her stepfather but from a man who seemed to have something to hide.

However, this time, Sarah didn't only have herself to consider. She was also responsible for Lilly.

In that moment, Sarah resolved to do everything in her power to keep the little girl safe.

CHAPTER ELEVEN

arah

DERMOT MCCOY SHOVED both of them into a small room at the back of his mountain cabin.

"Both of you will stay here." His eyes narrowed and his lips thinned. "I will be back in a few hours with food. Don't get any wise ideas about trying to escape. You won't like the consequences, trust me."

The large mountain man's eyes darkened dangerously and he stared her down.

Sarah swallowed, and pulled Lilly close to her side.

He left the room and closed the door firmly.

Sarah sighed in relief until she heard the lock click.

He had locked them both inside this small bedroom.

Panic began to well up in her throat. Her chest felt as if it would burst.

Terrible memories from her childhood, came back to haunt her. *When she had done something that made her stepfather angry — even something as simple as burning the food accidentally — she received a beating and was sent to her room.*

He would lock the door to her bedroom, telling her she needed to think about what she'd done. And he would see if she was better behaved by morning.

It seemed to be happening again, except this time she was an adult.

Her nerves tensed and a flicker of apprehension coursed through her as she looked at Lilly. The little girl was biting her lip and holding her dolly close to her heart.

Sarah went to her, worried about what this was doing to her.

"Don't worry. We will be okay. I promise I'll do everything I can to keep you safe." Sarah chose her words carefully, doing what she could to calm her and to create a peaceful atmosphere. "But, since we're here, we can play a game together or we could draw pictures if you'd like?"

Lilly nodded quickly. "A picture."

"Sure. I saw a small notebook and a pencil over here somewhere." Sarah grabbed the notebook and found two pencils. She gave one to Lilly. She desperately wanted to help this little girl feel like she was safe and that someone cared for her.

As Lilly started to draw, Sarah took her own paper and drew a picture of her and Dakota decorating the Christmas tree with Sarge lying near the tree.

When she glanced over at Lilly's picture, she saw a picture of an angry man with his hand raised up and a little girl who was running away from him. It looked like she was going towards a man and woman who stood in the corner of the picture.

Lilly looked over at Sarah and then pointing to the picture spoke softly. "I want my mama."

A tear slipped down the little girl's cheek.

Sarah moved to sit beside her, and embraced Lilly, holding her close to her heart.

"I know. We'll get you home soon." Sarah sighed and lowering her head, she kissed the little girl's hair. She didn't know how much she could promise Lilly, because Dermot McCoy had been acting so angry and unreasonable.

He was grandfather's friend who played chess with him sometimes over the years, but she had never seen him act like this.

It was almost as if Dermot was obsessed with his niece, to the point where he'd been willing to force the two of them back to his cabin at gunpoint.

What was really going on?

She was sure if her grandfather knew how his friend was acting, he would take him to task and call the Sheriff on him.

"I'm cold." Lilly whispered.

Sarah saw a small pile of clothes near the bed and reached for it. Searching through the small children's clothes, she grabbed a pink sweatshirt.

As she helped pull the sweatshirt over Lilly's head, once again she had a nagging sense about something in the back of her mind. There was something she should remember, but couldn't.

She hated that childhood trauma had stolen so much

from her.

Hugging the little girl in her arms, she determined to do her best to protect Lilly, whatever it took.

As Sarah looked around the small bedroom, she realized there wasn't any way to escape. The window in the room was small and higher up near the ceiling.

She wanted to leave. She wanted to take Lilly and run away from this cabin and go as far away from Dermot McCoy as she could get.

She wished she had her phone, angry at Dermot for forcing her to leave it back at her grandfather's cabin.

"I'm hungry." Lilly spoke softly and sat up. Sarah could hear the hunger pangs in her belly.

Sarah stole a quick glance at her watch and saw it had been more than three hours since Dermot had locked them in this room.

"Let's get out of here." Sarah knocked on the door to try to get the mountain man's attention, but he didn't answer. Perhaps he had decided to ignore them.

Sarah listened with her ear to the door, wondering what Dermot was up to.

With the exception of some rustling noises, there weren't other sounds coming from anywhere else in the cabin.

Had the mountain man left them all alone in the cabin?

She twisted the bracelet on her wrist as she agonized about what to do. She paced across the room, her face clouded with uneasiness. What if Dermot had left the two of them here alone?

Her fingers rubbed the key that was attached to the bracelet her mother gave her.

In that moment, mama's words came back to her memory. *This silver key has a special meaning. If you look closely, you see it's like a mirror. That reflection of you is the secret to open any door that's locked. Because the secret is inside you. You are courageous, smart and full of love. Remember that.*

A warmth flooded her along and she felt a new fire rising on the inside.

Looking down at the silver key she pondered Mama's words from so long ago. Twisting the slender old key between two fingers, all of a sudden an idea popped into her head.

Removing the key from the bracelet, she hurried to the door. Bending over she studied the key hole.

Slipping the long sled end of the key inside the doorknob, Sarah jiggled the key for a long time.

Without warning, she heard a click and was able to turn the doorknob.

Sarah stood up, surprised.

Turning to Lilly, she whispered. "I was able to open the door. Let's go see what's going on."

Reaching out, the little girl grabbed her hand and they walked down the hallway.

Sarah turned to Lilly with a finger to her closed lips. "We must be quiet, okay?"

Lilly nodded, her small fingers clutching her doll tighter to her chest.

They got to the kitchen and saw Dermot sitting on a chair by the kitchen table. Beer bottles were lined up and his head was tipped back, guzzling a new bottle.

In his other hand he held onto the gun and he sat there

staring at a picture he had propped up on the table in front of him.

In his half-drunk state Dermot stared accusingly at Sarah.

"Thought you were clever, huh? Somehow you managed to get yourselves out." He growled at them.

She shriveled a little at his expression. Lilly crept closer to her, squeezing her hand tightly.

Sarah replied in a low voice. "Lilly was hungry. Thought we could make some food."

The mountain man swayed a little in his chair as he eyed Lilly and her. With a quick nod, he waved the gun in his hand and pointed to the fridge. "Well then you can make something for all of us."

Sarah stumbled to the fridge, fear stabbing at her belly. Dermot's hand on that gun, made her nervous. She wasn't sure what sudden moves or mistakes he might make in his intoxicated state.

That alone set alarm bells ringing inside her.

Moving restlessly, she looked quickly through the contents in the fridge. She found leftover ham and spotted a loaf of bread on the kitchen counter. Hurriedly, she made ham sandwiches for each of them.

She placed the sandwiches on a plate and set them on the kitchen table.

Dermot eyed the food and with a shaky hand grabbed one of the sandwiches.

Sarah found a chair as far away from the mountain man as possible and Lilly came to sit on her lap.

They ate in silence.

Lilly's small body was shaking in fear. Sarah did her best to calm her, remembering all too well what it was like to be a child living in constant fear every day.

Sarah clenched her hands until her nails bit into her palm. A mixture of anger and fear flooded her body at the thought of living once again with an abusive man. But this time it was worse, because she had an innocent little girl she needed to protect.

She took a long deep breath, trying to force herself to relax.

At that moment Lilly spoke softly. "I have to go to the bathroom."

"All right. Come back here after, okay?" She didn't want Lilly to be by herself any longer than necessary in this strange man's house.

As Dermot's gaze switched between the two of them, the furrow between his brows grew deeper.

"Be quick about it." He growled and finished the half empty bottle in his hand.

Sarah was surprised that he still seemed to be in control of most of his senses, in spite of all the beer he'd consumed.

Finally, he picked up the picture on the table and held it in his shaking hand.

It looked like — for the time being at least — they were stuck with this angry mountain man. Somehow, Sarah found the courage to ask. "Who are those people in the photo?"

His angry eyes melted into a strange sadness as he stared at the picture.

"My wife and daughter. They died a few years ago. The doctors and police said it was an accident, but I know the truth. If it hadn't been for me, they'd be alive today."

The large mountain man's eyes moistened and he spoke with finality. "I am the one who killed them."

Sarah flinched at his words. Her hands, hidden from sight, twisted nervously. Fear gripped her.

She watched him warily as his emotions seemed to be in a precarious state.

Sarah desperately wanted answers, but something cautioned her not to ask any more questions.

All she knew for sure, was that somehow her and Lilly needed to escape, and quickly.

But, right now that was impossible.

DAKOTA STOOD to his feet and stretched, needing a break.

He had spent much of the afternoon trying to discover more details about the suspects he had on his list.

Walking to the kitchen he made himself a coffee.

Since, Sarah was away at her grandfather's cabin, he decided he would make the most of this time to dig deeper and find more clues and possible motives for each potential suspect.

Pouring himself a cup of coffee he reflected on what he'd uncovered so far.

He had a list of men who wore the boots with the star imprint, but hadn't really found much else.

They had learned that Sarah's stepfather wasn't involved in taking little Mindy after all.

That had surprised him. He'd been so sure that they were on the right track when they pursued Saul Bellans as the man responsible.

When the hospital confirmed Saul had been in the Hospital during the time Mindy went missing from her parent's home, the news had taken Dakota off guard.

Sarah's stepfather, wasn't the kidnapper after all.

Now, it seemed he was back to square one in his search.

Carrying his coffee mug back to his office, he looked around his desk at the scattered papers.

Hoping to clear his mind, he decided to clean up his office desk.

His dog moaned where he lay on the floor near the door.

Dakota grinned. "I couldn't agree more, Sarge. This pile of papers looks like a day's worth of work. It makes me tired just looking at it. I might be here all night."

Sarge lay down, sprawling out as if ready for a night's sleep.

Dakota shook his head and grinned. "You sleep and I'll get to work."

He got busy collecting the documents and stacking them into separate piles. Sometimes when he worked, things got a little messy.

Often when the piles of papers were cleaned up, he felt more clarity in his mind too. Strange how that worked, but it was something that helped him.

Finally, the last piece of paper was stacked in its proper place.

Glancing around his desk, he noticed a bunch of envelopes. Sarah had been getting the mail.

She set his mail on his desk faithfully, but he hadn't looked at any of the envelopes in three days.

Rifling through each envelope he saw lots of bills, which he set aside. However, one brown envelope caught his eye. On the return address was written Chase and Amanda Ballenger. Mindy's parents.

Curious as to why they would write to him, he opened the envelope.

Reaching inside, he pulled out photos with a little note attached. He sat down to read. *Dakota, we thought these pictures of our little girl might help you in your search. Praying for you to find Mindy quickly and bring her back home. Chase and Amanda Bellanger.*

Picking up each photo one by one he saw Mindy in different poses. One picture was taken with her parents by their living room fireplace. Another with her and her golden retriever dog. And the last one was taken of Mindy by herself.

The one detail that was common in each photo was that Mindy was holding a little doll close to her chest. The doll matched Mindy's own appearance, almost exactly. They both had big dark brown eyes and long wavy brown hair and each wore a pink shirt.

Looking again at each photo of Mindy, he became increasingly uneasy as something familiar in each photo nagged at him.

His gaze shifted to the doll she held in her arms.

Why did that doll look so familiar?

The doll seemed to have been specially ordered for

Mindy, because it looked almost exactly like the little girl — with very long brown hair and brown eyes.

Suddenly, he recalled where he'd seen that doll before.

The hair on the back of his neck stood on end, as the realization hit home.

The man by the cemetery had placed a doll similar to Mindy's by the child's gravesite.

Taking out his smartphone, he began to search through recent photos.

When he found the picture he had taken with the doll at the gravesite, he enlarged it so he could take a closer look.

As he compared the picture of the doll Mindy held in her arms to the doll at the gravesite, he was startled.

Both dolls looked exactly the same.

Looking again at the photo of the doll by the gravesite, the words etched in the stone were just barely visible.

Hannah Sophia McCoy beloved daughter.

McCoy.

His eyes widened. The shock of what he'd just discovered, hit him full force.

He'd just remembered whose little niece Sarah had gone to babysit.

Dakota dialed Sarah's phone number. *Please, answer quickly.*

He tried five times with no answer.

Fear tore at his insides.

Jumping to his feet, he hurried out to the hallway and grabbed his coat and slipped on his boots.

He rushed out of the house, his dog following at his heels.

I must save Sarah. And if that little girl is who I think she is, I must save her and bring her back safely to her parents.

He breathed out the words like a prayer as he drove as quickly as possible to Sarah's grandfather's cabin on the mountain.

CHAPTER TWELVE

arah

SARAH WAS STUNNED by Dermot McCoy's confession when she asked who was in the photo.

She stared wordlessly across the table from him, her heart pounding.

His words went around and around in her head.

My wife and daughter. They died a few years ago. The doctors and the police declared it to be an accident, but I know the truth. If it hadn't been for me, they would be alive today. I am the one who killed them.

In spite of the fact that he was feeling the effects of drinking too much, Sarah sensed there was some truth to his words.

Someone had told her years ago that sometimes the

most astounding truths were told when a person was on their sickbed or under the influence of drugs or alcohol.

Today, that statement had shown itself to be true again.

Now she sat there tense and filled with fear. Her composure was a fragile shell around her.

She needed something to do. She needed to keep busy so her mind wouldn't take her further down the path of fear.

Her gaze fell on the dirty plate lying on the kitchen table. Picking it up, she carried it to the kitchen.

She filled the sink and washed the dirty dishes, desperately needing to keep her hands working. Her mind was going in all sorts of directions.

The one thing that continued to circle in her mind, was the fact that this mountain man was obviously carrying some festering pain. However, the fact that he was hurting others needed to be stopped.

He desperately needed help.

As she finished scrubbing the last few dishes, she looked over to the front porch where the jackets and gloves hung. When she looked down, she noticed that Dermot's boots were placed upside down on a drying rack so that the boot's heel pointed upwards.

She halted, shaken at what she saw on the bottom of his boot. It was the star imprint. The same imprint Dakota had said the suspected kidnapper had on his boots.

Her body stiffened in shock as suddenly the puzzle pieces came together of the strange details that had been nagging at her memory.

The doll Lilly carried, was the same doll that Mindy

had in the picture Dakota carried. The pink shirt that Sarah found in Lilly's pile of clothes, was the same shirt Mindy wore in that picture also.

Mindy and Lilly were the same person. And Dermot McCoy was the man responsible for taking the little girl from her home.

A soft gasp escaped her, and she hurried to finish washing the dishes.

"Come sit back down." The mountain man's words were slurred.

Sarah put the last clean dish in the drying cloth and after drying her hands, slowly walked back to her chair.

She swallowed and willed her heart to stop racing.

Imposing an iron will on herself, she forced herself to remain calm and to look normal.

Sarah sat in the chair unmoving, unsure of what to say. What was there to say, when someone spoke of such terrible things they'd done in their lives? So she did what she'd always done, she waited for him to speak again.

She wasn't about to ask him how he killed his family, especially with that gun in his hand.

Dermot picked up the other photo that lay on the table, which was one of his wife and daughter standing outside in a garden. The little girl held a flower in one hand.

"My little girl Hannah's favorite flower was a lily." His gaze clouded with tears as he stared long and hard at the two women in the photo — the loved ones he'd lost.

Almost without warning, Dermot's tone changed abruptly. Sarah heard him speaking, but he seemed eerily in another world.

The photo of his wife shook as he held it in both hands. The big mountain man's voice broke. "Nellie, I wanted to make you happy ever since I married you. But, this time I did something that I'm afraid will make you very disappointed in me."

Laying the photo down on the table he traced the face of his dead wife with one finger.

"You know how happy we both were when our dear little daughter was born. As Hannah grew up into a little girl, one of the things I remember most was that she liked the lilies. She would run into the garden in the summer and bring flowers into the house. It made us all so happy."

She heard the permanent sorrow in his voice that seemed to weigh him down.

Forcing herself to keep silent, she waited to hear the rest of his story.

"I was just missing our own little Hannah so much, that I went searching for someone who looked like our little girl. I found Mindy in Colorado. She looked so similar to Hannah so I brought her home. I thought it would make us a family again. But it didn't seem to turn out the way I wanted it to."

Sarah sucked in a breath at his words.

A new realization hit her that Dermot McCoy wasn't really thinking straight. Had he been so weighed down by grief and guilt that he started to re-create the reality he once had?

Her fears increased.

What would he do next?

At that moment, Lilly — er, Mindy — walked down the hallway towards her.

At the same time, the door to the cabin crashed open and Dakota came rushing into the room, his dog at his heels.

Dermot McCoy swayed to his feet and grabbed his gun. Grabbing Sarah's arm, he pulled her towards him.

Panic was rioting within her. How would they get out of this mess?

With wide eyes she looked over to Dakota and then at Mindy.

Sarah feared the little girl would get caught in the middle. So, she called out. "Mindy, run to the door."

Sarah pointed to the porch and hoped the little girl would obey her instructions.

For a moment, Mindy stopped looking confused, but when she saw Sarah pointing to the door, she ran so she was just behind Dakota.

"Sarge, protect!" Dakota spoke firmly to his dog and Sarah watched as Sarge stood by Mindy like a fierce four-legged warrior.

Sarah breathed a sigh of relief that Mindy was safe.

All of sudden, Dermot tightened his grip on her and pulled her against his chest.

A strong odor of beer and sweat lingered on his breath and on his body. He swayed, unsteadily on his feet while trying to hold onto Sarah at the same time.

Sarah released an audible gasp as panic flooded her belly and quickly spread up to her chest, confining her airways so she could hardly breathe.

"Drop the gun, McCoy!" Dakota's low voice commanded. He held the gun in his hand pointed directly at Dermot McCoy.

Dakota's clenched jaw tightened in determination. His dark eyes stared at Dermot with an icy resolve.

The mountain man wobbled back and forth, unsteady on his feet and doing his best to hold onto Sarah. Still he held his gun pointed at her.

"I need Sarah to stay here to help take care of Lilly. If I drop the gun, you'll take her."

Dakota frowned at McCoy's words. "What?"

"He has renamed Mindy and calls her Lilly." Sarah tried to explain, but Dermot silenced her with a jerk.

Dakota stepped closer, with his gun still pointed at the mountain man. "Let me be clear. Neither Mindy or Sarah will stay here with you McCoy. Drop the gun now, or you will face even worse charges against you. Trust me, you won't like the consequences."

Dermot staggered on his feet and suddenly dropped the gun.

It landed on the floor with a thud.

Dakota hurried and kicked the gun, shoving it to the other side of the kitchen before the mountain man would have a chance to grab it.

Sarah released a breath of relief and ran to Mindy who stood in the doorway of the porch, holding her doll tight to her chest.

Dakota was just putting handcuffs on Dermot McCoy, when Sheriff Turnbull and two officers entered the cabin.

"Dakota, looks like you found your guy after all." The Sheriff eyed Dermot McCoy and nodded. "Good."

The Sheriff motioned for the two officers with him. "Read Mister McCoy his rights and then haul him to the police station."

Sarah hugged Mindy closer to her, so grateful the little girl was now safe.

Sheriff Turnbull turned to Dakota. "Looks like that list of suspects you had was spot on. Must be all that FBI training you've had that helped you solve this one."

Dakota shrugged. "The FBI training was only partially responsible. Most of the help I've had on this case came from former P.I. Art Mulreedy and from my lovely wife."

"Having good people on your team is invaluable. I'm glad you managed to get this one solved, Dakota." The Sheriff slapped his shoulder. "I might ask you for more details later."

The Sheriff left the cabin, following his officers to the police cruiser that waited outside.

Mindy decided to sit down and began playing with her doll. Sarge continued to stay close by the little girl's side.

Sarah turned back to Dakota, only to see his dark earnest eyes seeking hers.

He walked towards her, his eyes hooded like those of a hawk.

As he stepped closer, she could feel familiar emotions rise up on the inside.

She had just been through a harrowing experience, which included being held hostage.

Her nerves were fraying at the edges.

"Are you okay?" His hands reached out, squeezing her shoulders gently as his dark eyes intently scanned her face.

Sarah nodded. "For the most part."

She was doing her best to remain calm outwardly, even though inside her emotions were like a rollercoaster.

The tender concern in his eyes was almost her undoing.

She swallowed back emotions and in a hoarse voice said. "We made it through safe and sound. So we're okay."

Dakota rubbed the back of his neck. "I panicked when I finally realized what happened. I knew I needed to find you and get you to safety."

Pulling her into his arms, her husband held her close, breathing a sigh of relief. She couldn't help but be surprised at the anxiety she heard in his voice.

Her heart jolted and her pulse pounded as his arms wrapped around her. She could feel his rapid heartbeat in his chest as he held her close.

Her instinctive response to him was so powerful.

Every time she saw Dakota it seemed her feelings for him intensified. She wanted to love him — but it seemed at every turn he distanced himself from her.

He rejected her love.

She couldn't allow her heart to ache with longing anymore for a man who wouldn't allow himself to love her.

She needed to be strong.

Pushing against his chest, she stepped back.

"Thank you Dakota." Sarah forced a smile. She fixed her eyes on the little girl before turning back to Dakota. "Mindy and I are grateful for all you did to protect us."

For a moment he studied her, confusion lingering on his features before he nodded. "Welcome."

As Sarah helped Mindy with her coat, she fought to control her swirling emotions.

Dakota looked confused by her, but so was she. She wanted… well, what she really wanted she couldn't have.

All of her loneliness and confusion welded together in one upsurge of devouring yearning.

She would have to steel her heart against her fake husband. Sarah didn't know how she would conquer her involuntary reactions to those rare moments when Dakota used that gentle loving look on her.

If she didn't resist him, she believed her heart would shatter into a million tiny pieces.

DAKOTA EXPELLED a long breath as he parked the truck in front of the Refuge Mountain Motel.

Looking over at Sarah and Mindy, he couldn't help but feel relief that they were safe from the clutches of Dermot McCoy.

Sarah was safe. That was all that mattered.

He stopped for a moment and inhaled a quick breath. It hit him suddenly, that his feelings for his wife were far deeper than he ever thought possible.

Dakota knew he loved her.

Turning towards him, she asked. "Are you ready for this?"

Heat crawled up his neck to his cheeks.

He was so busy thinking about Sarah, that he forgot what the mission was for today. The plan was that Amanda and Chase Bellanger were to meet him at this Motel to reunite with their daughter.

They had already talked with the police and would talk

to them again later, but this meeting for their family, needed to take place somewhere normal where little Mindy wouldn't be frightened.

"Yeah." Dakota turned to Mindy. "Grab your doll, Mindy. Someone is waiting outside for you."

He helped the little girl out of his truck and took her by the hand. With Sarah on her other side they walked to the room where her parents were located. Sarge followed at Mindy's heels, staying close by her side.

Both parents must have seen their daughter through the window, because they came rushing out the door.

"Oh Mindy, I'm so happy to hold you in my arms again. That you're here, safe and sound. I love you." Mindy's mother got to her knees and held out her arms.

"Mama!" Tears streamed down Mindy's cheeks as she ran into her mother's arms.

For several long minutes the two hugged and cried together, happy to finally be together again.

Mindy's tearful reunion with her parents was beautiful to watch.

For Dakota it was always an incredible feeling when another child was found.

"It never gets old."

"What?" Sarah turned to him, wiping a tear from her cheek.

Dakota pointed at Mindy and both parents now all hugging each other — a family united once more.

Sarah nodded. "I'm so glad she's okay and finally going home. That will be so wonderful for her, but there will still be healing from trauma. I know all about that."

"I know you do, Sarah. I'm sorry you had to go through so much of that kind of pain and abuse."

Dakota wrapped his arm around her shoulders, wanting to take away the pain of all she endured.

Chase and Amanda walked towards them, Mindy holding tightly to her mother's hand.

"Thank you for finding our little girl. We thought we'd lost her. Thank you so much. You don't know how much this means to us." Amanda hugged him and Sarah both.

Dakota's heart brimmed over with happiness to see the family together at last. "I'm very glad we found your daughter and were able to bring her back to the place where she belongs. Home."

Chase's eyes were glistening with unshed tears as he shook Dakota's hand. "It means the world to us that you brought her back. Thank you."

Dakota squeezed the father's hand and nodded. "Welcome."

Amanda wiped more tears from her cheeks and said softly. "We're going to go have some family time now, I think."

Dakota nodded. "Well deserved family time."

They waved to the Bellangers and watched them walk into their motel room. Sarge stayed by Dakota's side, watching Mindy walk away with her family.

"It's okay boy. I know you lost a friend today, but you still have me." Dakota smiled and turned to Sarah.

Dark shadows were under her eyes.

"We should head home too."

They got into the truck and Dakota started heading toward the ranch.

"Don't you need to stop and talk to the Sheriff?" Sarah asked.

Dakota shrugged. "It can wait until tomorrow. You've been through enough today. It's more important that you are home — some place where you feel safe and where you can rest."

Sarah leaned her head back on the passenger seat and sighed.

He realized she must be exhausted from the day. There was silence between them until they arrived home.

As they entered the cabin, his dog ran ahead to his food and water bowl.

Dakota turned to Sarah. "Want to have a mug of hot chocolate with me before you head to bed?"

She hesitated for a moment, before she nodded. "That sounds good."

By the time Dakota brought the steaming mugs into the living room, his dog had his head on Sarah's lap and she was rubbing his furry head.

Dakota shook his head as he handed the mug to Sarah.

"Sarge looks quite comfortable beside you." Dakota eyed his dog, thinking he wouldn't mind trading places with his dog right about now.

Sarge was getting the attention from his wife that he wanted for himself.

Dakota sat on the comfy recliner across from Sarah and eyed her with concern. "I know you'll want to go to bed soon, but do you want to talk about what happened?"

Sarah sighed and set her mug down on the coffee table. "I think I'm just frustrated with myself that I didn't realize right away that Lilly was actually Mindy."

"It's okay. Lilly had short red hair, whereas in the photo you saw of Mindy, she had long brown hair. Anyone could have made that mistake." Dakota reasoned calmly.

Sarah sighed. "I suppose. The doctor told me that because of the trauma from my childhood, I might forget details sometimes, especially in high stress situations. It was certainly true today."

"Healing from trauma takes a little bit of time."

Sarah shrugged. "I know."

"I think sometimes we can have memories that need to be healed." Dakota thought of the memories around his little sister that still haunted him.

Without thinking, he started talking about it.

"Throughout the years I've wondered what my own sister had to endure when she was kidnapped." He shook his head, sighing heavily. "The police never found her."

"I'm so sorry, Dakota." She reached for his hand and squeezed it gently.

He held her soft hand in his, shocked by the electricity of her touch.

"It's okay." He lowered his head for a moment, as tears pricked at the back of his eyes. "I know you understand. I think sometimes that the burden of what happened to my sister is too heavy to think about. I go crazy when I let my thoughts linger on it."

Sarah nodded. "I understand. It's better not to let your mind go there. If you keep thinking about the 'what ifs' eventually they'll drive you crazy because you can't go back and fix what happened."

Dakota nodded. "Most of the time I blame myself for

what happened to her. If I had been more alert that day, my sister would never have been kidnapped."

"Oh, Dakota. That kind of blame and regret is too great a burden to bear." Sarah squeezed his hand, her green eyes filling with tears. "You have to forgive yourself of any blame you've put on yourself and let it go."

Dakota turned her hand in his, loving its softness. "You sound like my mother."

"She's a wise woman."

"Yes, she is. And so are you, Sarah." Dakota took a deep breath. There was so much he wanted to tell her. "You've been an amazing friend all these years, listening to me and giving me advice. But ever since we started this fake marriage, I feel like our friendship has gone much deeper…"

Unexpectedly, Sarah interrupted him and stood to her feet. "I appreciate your friendship too, Dakota." She carried their mugs to the kitchen and he followed her. She continued talking. "But, I'm glad you brought up our fake marriage."

She turned around suddenly. "Because I have some news to tell you."

Dakota lifted an eyebrow, suddenly sensing a strange foreboding.

"I talked with my grandfather, and he's moving to town by the end of the week. In fact, he and Mrs. Moore have decided they want to marry. So, I will move in with my grandfather and help him plan his wedding, and you can have your cabin back to yourself." Sarah explained calmly.

"You won't need to be bothered by our fake marriage

for much longer. We can get an annulment and I will be out of your life." At Sarah's announcement, a strange painful ache began in his belly.

"Why?"

"That was our agreement. I was to help you find the kidnapper and you were to help me convince my grandfather to move to town. After that, the fake marriage would be over." Sarah straightened the towel by the kitchen sink and turning to him said.

"It looks like you'll soon be free of me and can go back to living your life without all the extra commitments, just how you want it to be."

Sarah leaned over a kissed his cheek. "Thank you for all you have done to help me Dakota."

She turned and left the kitchen before he could say anything.

He thought about Sarah's words, and a new awareness hit him.

He didn't want to be free of commitment. He didn't want to be free of this marriage. He didn't want to be free of the woman he loved.

Sarah was that woman.

Now, when he finally realized the truth, was he about to lose her?

Sarah

SLIPPING HER BOOTS ON, Sarah put the knitted hat on her head and put the matching gloves on her hands.

Her grandmother had made them and she treasured them.

With only five days to go until Christmas, the weather had turned snowy and she wanted to keep warm.

Grandfather limped to the small porch with her dog following close behind. "I thought I heard you slipping your boots on. Where are you going?

"The quilting bee at *A Goode Yarn,* grandfather." Sarah wound the scarf around her neck and smiled warmly at her grandfather. "I mentioned it this morning at breakfast, remember?"

He shrugged. "I don't remember. But, have fun."

"I'll be gone for a few hours, so don't wait up for me, okay?" Sarah didn't want him to stay up late waiting and worrying for her.

Maisie rubbed up against her leg, trying to get her attention. Sarah scratched behind her ears before walking to her grandfather.

After giving him a hug, Sarah reached up to kiss his weathered cheek. "See you later."

Sarah left the house and hurried down the sidewalk, happy to be able to meet with her quilting friends again.

Minutes later, she entered the yarn shop and saw Lynda Goode, the store's owner, setting up coffee and tea on the large table in the corner of the room.

"Sarah, you're here. Some of the women came early to chat before we get to stitching. Grab yourself a tea or coffee and join them." Lynda pointed towards the women who were sitting on the sofas and chairs, sipping hot drinks and talking.

"Thanks Lynda, I will." Sarah unwrapped her scarf and took off her hat and gloves as she walked towards the women.

CoraLee turned to her, giving her a big hug. "I was thinking about you today." Her friend grabbed Sarah's hand and pulled her towards another set of couches where it was more private.

"So, tell me what's going on. You and Dakota just sent a kidnapper to jail and you saved an innocent child's life. Now, you're living with your grandfather. What's happened between the two of you?" A puzzled concern crossed her friend's face.

Sarah's voice broke miserably. "We had agreed on a

fake marriage until my grandfather moved to town. And since he has now moved here, our agreement is over."

CoraLee squeezed her hand. "If it's over between the two of you, why do you look so miserable?"

Sarah shrugged and a pain squeezed her heart as she thought of Dakota.

"Because, I still love him and it might take me a while to get over him." A permanent sorrow seemed to weigh her down. "And he doesn't love me. He only sees me as a good friend, nothing more. And I can't spend my life with a man who doesn't love me."

"I understand. Maybe you haven't heard all of his side of the story." Her friend sipped her tea before asking. "Isn't there any way you two could talk some more?"

Sarah sighed. "Well, Dakota texted me and asked if I would go riding horses with him tomorrow like we used to. He said there was a lot he needed to tell me."

"And..." Her friend always knew when she was worried.

"And I'm not sure if meeting with Dakota is a good idea. I seem to lose control of my senses when I'm with him." Sarah closed her eyes reliving that final scene with Dakota, once again feeling the loss.

"I really think you should go talk to him and hear what he has to say." CoraLee studied her for a moment. "That might not be what you wanted to hear, but I honestly think it's a good idea. You need to hear him out, Sarah and I'm confident he will listen to what you have to say too."

Sarah shifted in her chair a moment, before nodding. "I suppose you're right. I should at least talk with him and hear what he has to say."

"Yep. You might be pleasantly surprised."

Sarah tossed her friend a smile that was without humor. What did Dakota want to say to her?

A nagging worry bothered her as the ladies gathered to quilt. The one bit of happiness was that she was with ladies she adored and together they were stitching a wedding quilt for her grandfather and his bride-to-be.

The colors were her grandfather and Mrs. Moore's favorites. Blue, green and yellow were mixed together as rings were interwoven throughout the large quilt.

Sarah had dreamed of a wedding memory quilt of her own one day when she married — this time for real.

She longed for a man who would truly love her with all his heart. A man who would want to marry her.

Sarah had a feeling that it would take a long time, after the marriage between her and Dakota was annulled, before she would be willing to fall in love again.

However, first she would need to hear what Dakota had to say tomorrow. Uncertainty and anxiousness clawed in her belly.

Sarah only hoped that when he talked to her, she would be able to sheath her inner feelings.

But, hiding her feelings from him, was as unlikely to happen as Dakota telling her he loved her.

DAKOTA RODE HIS GELDING, matching his pace with Sarah's mare.

He couldn't help but be surprised when she showed up to the ranch.

He fully expected her to turn down his invitation. In fact, from the last time he'd seen Sarah, he expected her to run in the other direction.

It was as much as he deserved. He could admit that.

However, he wanted to fix things between them. That was why he was single-mindedly focused on talking with Sarah.

As their horses reached the top of the mountain, he turned to look at her.

His heart jolted and his pulse pounded just being near her. Would she accept him?

Dakota stopped his horse near an out-cropping of three pine trees located near the waterfall.

It was the same place they had rode their horses together a few different times throughout the years.

However, the last time they'd been here together, it hadn't ended so well.

That was another thing for which he needed to apologize to Sarah.

Slipping off his horse, he tied him loosely to the tree.

He turned to help Sarah, but she was already on the ground, leading her mare to tie her up.

"Thank you for agreeing to ride with me today." Together they walked closer to the falls.

"I find I'm very curious about what you want to talk about. I thought we had said everything there was to say last time we were together." Sarah's wide green eyes looked up at him, troubled.

He turned to her, a furrow between his brows. "The last time we were together at the ranch, I was still trying to process the kidnapping along with trying to figure out what was happening between us. I'm sorry, for being abrupt and impatient with you Sarah."

Sarah swallowed and looked down for a moment, before lifting up vulnerable green eyes to him. "It was a tough day for all of us, wasn't it? I forgive you. Is that what you wanted to talk about?"

"No. There's much more." Dakota spotted the log tree where they had often sat in the past.

Wiping the snow off the top, he reached his hand. "Come, let's sit together and talk."

Sarah had a wary look on her face as she sat on the log beside him. It was the kind of expression she wore when she was worried about something.

"I wanted to tell you more about my story. I've never told anyone the real difficult parts before, so this is a first for me." Dakota looked at her, and seeing a warm smile hovering over her lips, he began.

Sarah said. "I have always hoped you would tell me more about yourself."

He nodded, knowing the truth of her words. Even from eleven years old, Sarah had always been pestering him with questions about how he had been adopted and what happened to his birth family.

"Before I was adopted by Mack and Annie Callahan, my family was my sister, my mom and me. I hardly remember my dad, because he died when I was only three years old from an accident at work. We later found out, he was drinking too much."

Sarah turned, listening intently.

"It was my mom, my sister and me. My mom was of American Lakota Indian heritage and sometimes she had a difficult time finding jobs. Her brother and father didn't want her back on their tribe, because she had married my Irish father. So, she stayed away." Dakota sighed heavily.

"After my dad died, mom was sad a lot. But she still encouraged my sister and I to do things together and have fun." Dakota smiled. "I remember the day my mom took this picture, like it was yesterday."

He pulled out the photo of the two of them from his pocket.

Sarah looked at it and smiled. "You are both covered in mud."

"Yeah." Memories swirled around Dakota of that day. "I was playing outside with my little sister, waiting for mom to come home from work. Cheyenne had been chasing me, eager to put a worm down my shirt, just like I'd done to her. It had rained the day before, which was why we were covered in mud."

"Then without warning, my mom stepped into the backyard. Seeing our faces, she laughed and hurriedly grabbed her camera and snapped this photo." Dakota grinned. "Of course, as soon as I was distracted that's when Cheyenne saw her chance and sneakily slid a worm down the back of my shirt. I was jumping up and down trying to get rid of it and my little sister was laughing at me, when Mom snapped the photo."

Sarah grinned. "That's a great memory."

"It was." He rubbed his forehead as memories came back. "It was only a few days later that someone kidnapped Cheyenne out of our backyard. I was taking care of her whenever my mom worked. She worked full-time and I was the one that needed to watch her. I was the protective older brother. And I loved her. But I failed her. My little sister was gone."

He swallowed back emotion and he felt Sarah's small hand slip gently into his.

"I'm so sorry, Dakota. That's a terrible thing to live through." Sarah's gentleness almost undid him. "Did the police search for her?"

"Yeah." He sighed. "In spite of their best efforts, they couldn't find her. My mom became so depressed and heartsick at the loss of her daughter and earlier her husband, that she died less than a year later. The doctor said it was pneumonia, but I will always believe my mom died of a broken heart."

He blinked back moisture from his eyes and looked down at his feet.

Sarah sat closer to him and leaned her head on his shoulder. "I'm so sorry for all your loss, Dakota. Nobody should have to go through so much heartache and loss."

Dakota grimaced. "For years, it's been difficult to process all this grief and sorrow. You're the first one I've told the whole story to."

"Thank you for trusting me enough to share it, Dakota." Sarah squeezed her hand and he squeezed back. "Sometimes, when we talk about our grief with others, it helps to lift the burden a little."

Dakota nodded. "Yeah. That feels true."

They sat in silence for a few moments. They had always been able to be comfortable with silence between them. Sarah always seemed to sense what he needed.

"The reason I wanted to tell you that story was so it would help you to understand me better." Dakota's voice was hoarse and raw. "You see, I've always had a very difficult time getting close to a woman. Simply, because the women I loved in the past, I failed them. Memories haunt me still, how I couldn't stop my sister from being kidnapped or my mother from dying."

I was really made aware of it, when you were forced to Dermot McCoy's cabin."

Dakota squeezed her hand as he remembered the panic that swept through his body. "When the puzzle pieces began coming together that you were babysitting Mindy, I knew you wouldn't be safe from this terrible man who would take a little girl. The worst part was that I wasn't there to protect you. I panicked and hurried as fast as I could to your grandfather's cabin."

"But I wasn't there."

"Yeah. Fear overwhelmed me and I rushed to McCoy's cabin. I was sure I was too late." All the feelings rushed back through Dakota as he remembered.

"Sarah." Dakota ground out her name as though in torment and reached for his wife, hauling her into his arms with the force of his need. All his pent-up fears and worries suddenly came crashing down on him.

"I thought I'd lost you. I nearly went mad with fear. I can't bear to go through that again."

Sarah's wide eyes were filled with moisture as her gaze met his. "But you weren't too late. And you did protect me and Mindy."

Dakota swallowed back the emotion that threatened to consume him. He pulled her onto his lap, showering kisses on her forehead, nose and cheeks. "I finally realized that day, when I nearly lost you, how much you mean to me."

Finally, he leaned his forehead against hers. "Yeah. I'm so thankful I was able to get there in time, because I don't know if I could make it without you, Sarah."

His chest heaved and Dakota closed his eyes trying to force back the vivid images at seeing Sarah held captive by Dermot McCoy with his gun pointed at her head.

Dakota released a jagged breath as he stroked her hair. "Since we began this fake marriage, you've changed my world."

"What do you mean?"

"You've made cinnamon buns and cooked meals and made my lonely cabin a welcoming home. You bring cheer to everyone and light everywhere that you go. And I don't know how I've lived this long without you by my side. I need you in my life, Sarah."

Her eyes widened and moistened with unshed tears all at the same time. "I believe you mean it."

"I do mean it, with every beat of my heart." Dakota pressed his lips against the top of her head.

&.

SARAH SWALLOWED back the emotion lodged in her throat.

Dakota needed her and wanted her to stay by his side.

Just when she'd given up all hope, he confessed his longing for her.

She burrowed deeper into his arms.

In this moment, she sensed a deeper connection to

Dakota, almost like they bonded in a way they hadn't before.

Her husband had told her that he needed her, but it was only now that she'd finally believed him.

"I'm sorry for how I've pushed you away for such a long time." Dakota's gruff whisper broke through the stillness of the moment.

"I understand now why you kept you guard up." Sarah remembered the story of his mother and sister, still feeling his deep sorrow.

He kissed her head and pulled her close. "It's true. For years, the weight of my mother and sister's death has all but broken me. I'm scared that somehow, I'll repeat similar mistakes with you. I can't lose you. Not now, when I've finally found you.

"And your fears?" Sarah needed to hear him say the words, because this had been a big part of the struggle between them for a long time.

Dakota turned his dark eyes on her, and the smoldering flame she saw in his eyes startled her.

He expelled a labored breath. "I have decided to stop hiding in fear, and I want to spend a lifetime learning how to love you, Sarah."

Tears of pleasure found their way to her eyes at his words.

She turned to look into Dakota's dark eyes.

"You love me?" There was a deep need inside Sarah to hear this man say those three important words.

"I do. I think I started to fall in love with you when we searched for that Christmas tree. That kiss we shared, hasn't left me thoughts since that day and I realized that I was deeply, recklessly in love with you, Sarah." Dakota's arms tightened around her, and she enjoyed every moment of his attention.

Sarah cherished hearing Dakota's words of love. "I love you too, with all my heart."

Dakota turned her towards him, his dark gaze looking intently downward on her lips. "I have enjoyed your friendship for years, but the woman you have become now is beyond compare. You are kind, compassionate and selfless. And you also happen to be enchantingly beautiful."

Her heart jolted and her pulse pounded at his words and she looked up to meet his gaze.

Dakota kissed both of her cheeks, looking downward at her lips. "Before I kiss you, I want to ask you a question."

"What?"

Dakota hesitated and pulled back slightly so he could look deeply into her eyes.

"Originally, we agreed to a fake marriage, but things have changed. Today, we've realized we're in love."

Dakota swallowed nervously, before he spoke again. "What do you think about us getting married for real?"

Her cheeks colored under the heat of his gaze.

The revelation of his love for her mingled with his need to have her by his side for a lifetime, was what she most needed to hear. "Dakota, I would be honored to be your real wife."

Smiling, and with her heart in her eyes Sarah continued. "You have protected me, trusted me to tell me your story, and have truly honored me with your love. I would be proud to be your wife."

"I love you, Dakota."

At her whispered words her husband's lips were suddenly on hers, turning, twisting, tasting, as if he needed to know for sure that their love was real.

When he finally let her go, Sarah was weak and trembling. She looked up at him, feeling vulnerable at the effect his kisses had on her.

His large hands reached up to push aside a tendril of hair that had fallen in front of her eyes. His dark eyes searched hers intently, a hesitation in his movements.

Sarah leaned over and softly brushed her lips against his, her kiss saying more than words ever could.

Dakota sighed and folded her in his arms. "Sarah, I can't believe you are mine. My beautiful wife. Let me show you how much I love you."

He reclaimed her lips, crushing her to him with the longing of a man who had been denied her kisses for much too long.

Suddenly, his kisses changed. His lips touched hers as tender and light as a summer breeze.

Sarah felt transported on a soft, wispy cloud.

Melting into Dakota's arms, his kisses branded her once more with the promise of love that would last a lifetime.

EPILOGUE

Christmas Eve...

DAKOTA

DAKOTA LOOKED out over the crowd gathered in the Community Church, a nervous smile hovering on his lips.

He could hardly believe he was about to marry Sarah, for real this time. She had asked him if they could get married again at church, with everyone who wanted to come in attendance.

She wanted to celebrate their love and the start of their very real marriage.

He agreed, willing to do anything to make her happy.

Many folks had come tonight to support them, it was a little overwhelming.

He had talked with Sarah, and they had agreed to marry just before the Christmas Eve service. That way most of their friends and family could be there to celebrate with them.

The joyful ringing of Church Bells in the tower of the Community Church, brought a long sigh of contentment to his heart.

His parents used to say Christmas was about hope, miracles and love. Standing here today, he would have to agree.

All three virtues were wrapped up in his lovely bride, Sarah.

Surprised, Dakota realized he couldn't remember feeling this happy in a really long time.

He owed this newfound happiness to the fact that he'd been given a second chance at love with the one woman he adored.

Simply being in Sarah's presence gave him so much joy.

Playing his guitar softly in the background, his brother Denver crooned a love song he'd written. Many folks in the crowd were gently moving side-to-side along with his country tune.

Denver reminded him he had agreed to sing for their wedding because he believed in the power of love… especially for those who were given a second chance.

Scanning the front row of the church, Dakota smiled warmly at the sight of his brothers and wives and families sitting there.

His mom was grinning from ear to ear, always thrilled when another one of her sons married.

He wished his dad could have been here to see this day. Memories returned of the letters Mack Callahan had written to each of his sons. In his letter to Dakota, he had hinted at a Christmas wedding between him and Sarah.

At the time, Dakota had shoved the idea aside, believing that his dad was dreaming of something that could never happen.

Dakota looked heavenward. *Thanks, Dad for always believing in me. Thank you for writing those encouraging words that I should try for a second time, to win Sarah's heart. As it turns out, you were right after all.*

Sarah has always been the one woman I loved, and today she is becoming my wife for real this time. I don't deserve her, but I'm grateful for the second chance at love. So, if you can hear me from up there, I just want to say thank you.

Looking towards the back of the church, he saw the maid of honor waiting at the double doors.

CoraLee began to walk down the aisle. She wore a dark red velvet evening dress that suited her slender figure. Her long brown hair was back in a French braid with baby's breath intertwined throughout the silk waves.

Hunter who stood beside him as best man, watched CoraLee intently. He decided he would need to tease him later about his attraction to Sarah's maid of honor.

All of a sudden, the music changed and folks stood to their feet for one person: *his bride.*

Sarah walked so gracefully down the aisle that she seemed to glide.

With one hand curved into her grandfather's arm, her smile brightened as she neared the front of the church where he waited.

Dakota was awestruck by how beautiful his bride looked.

She was wearing her grandmother's gown the same one she wore for their fake marriage.

But, somehow everything about his bride seemed more radiant today.

Sarah was happier than he'd ever seen her and it seemed like she glowed.

Reverend Jon, stood at the front near him. He wore a calm smile of serenity and peace, which was sorely needed for today.

As Sarah walked towards him, he couldn't help but be reminded of the time they spent on the mountain.

The first time they had rode their horses to the waterfall, he had hurt Sarah. His pulling away from her, had caused her not to trust him.

A few days ago, when he had apologized for the many times he had hurt her and bared his heart to her, she had graciously forgiven him.

Her words of love in return, had been like a healing balm to all the wounded places in his heart.

And today she would be his *forever*.

Her grandfather placed Sarah's hand in Dakota's, looking at him intently for a moment.

Dakota nodded. He knew what her grandfather was asking him without any words passing between them. *My granddaughter is all I have left in the world. Treat her with kindness and love. Take care of her like the most precious treasure that she is.*

And he would. He would protect her and love her as his most precious treasure for the rest of his life.

Reverend Jon spoke of marriage for a few minutes before he asked them to say their marriage vows.

Looking into Sarah's beautiful green eyes, he poured his heart into words that would bind them together forever.

"When I first saw you, you were ten years old and as skittish as a filly who had been mishandled once too often. Yet, you were determined to show me that you weren't a little girl, that you could ride horses and handle yourself just like a grown up."

"And grow up you did. You became a beautiful woman. But along the way, I realized something important. Your courage and compassion to care for stray animals or people and to do the right thing, has won me over since the first day I met you."

"Now you are even more beautiful, with an even bigger heart. We've shared the good and the bad between us over the years, and we became closer. Sadly, fear of love held me back from accepting your love for a time. But you won me over. It was your acceptance, forgiveness and love gave me and us a new start. Now, I truly see for the first time the amazing treasure that you are. I look forward to making more memories in our future together. I love you, Sarah."

Sarah's wide green eyes glistened with emotion and her steady gaze captivated him, seeming to stare straight into his soul.

Now, they were married in truth.

What they had together was no longer fake, but wonderfully real. Today was the first day they were starting their marriage based on love and commitment.

Gathering her into his arms, he held her close to his heart.

His arms encircled her waist and he lowered his head, gently placing his lips on hers.

Her sweet kiss captivated him and nearly took his breath away. Dakota breathed deeply of the scent of roses all around his bride, and loved the way she clung to him.

Holding Sarah close in his arms, Dakota realized that he'd finally found the place where he belonged and was truly loved.

At long last, he'd come home.

SARAH QUIVERED at the sweet tenderness of her husband's kiss. Her pulse quickened as Dakota's warm lips pressed against her own.

His love had melted her heart and she was more in love with him than ever before.

It seemed she had waited such a long time for Dakota. For years she had longed to marry a man who would love her wholly and completely.

This forever kind of love had been her focus from the beginning, but in all honesty, she never thought it would happen for her.

All of the cruel words her stepfather had spoken to her during her childhood, she had come to believe.

However, believing that she wasn't worthy to be loved or that she was only someone others felt sorry for, had been all lies. Believing those lies had created open wounds in her heart. So she had built up walls of protection so she wouldn't get hurt.

She saw it all so clearly now.

Dakota had helped her, protected her and believed in her, when she didn't believe in herself.

He truly did love her.

Sarah's heart overflowed with happiness.

Today, in marrying Dakota, she would truly belong to a large family. For so many years, she had felt unwanted and lost. And she'd given up hope that would ever change.

Now, her and Dakota would begin their own family and as a bonus, she would also become part of the Callahan family.

Her dreams of love and belonging were coming true, and it was the most incredible feeling in the world.

Dakota slowly removed his lips from hers, his dark eyes shining with tenderness and love.

As he stepped back, Sarah found she missed her husband's warmth.

The pastor announced them as husband and wife. Dakota grabbed her hand and they walked down the aisle toward the back of the church.

Sarah fingered her mustard seed necklace, remembering the words of her beloved grandmother.

She looked outward toward the sky and whispered heavenward. *Grandmother, you told me that a tiny mustard seed of faith moves mountains. You were right. There have quite a few details in my life where I've needed to hold onto faith.*

The biggest one being that I would marry the man I love. I hope you're smiling down from heaven, because I'm happy to tell you I married Dakota today. So, if you're listening, I just want to say thank you.

As they reached the back of the church, Dakota pulled her close and kissed the top of her head.

"I'm still so amazed that you agreed to my wife for real this time, Sara Callahan." Dakota smiled wide his dark eyes filled with promises.

"And I'm happy to be your wife, Dakota Callahan." Sarah turned to him, with all the love she had in her heart.

"Okay you two. I know you love each other, but it's time to focus on some of your guests for a minute." CoraLee walked up to them and hugged them. Following behind her, Sarah noticed a few members of their weekly quilting bee.

"You have our attention, for now." Dakota turned to her friend and winked.

CoraLee offered him a wry grin and handed Sarah the quilt in her hands. "All of us from the quilting bee, have a little something we wanted to give you two, to celebrate your wedding."

Sarah reached the quilt and held it up, letting the long length fall to the floor. "It's a photo memory quilt. This is so beautiful."

The quilt was made from photos of both Dakota's and Sarah's life. It was made like a film strip that surrounded the sides of the blanket. Pictures from when they were babies and up until their adult years were included.

Sarah recognized photos that her grandmother had taken when Sarah and Dakota used to go horse riding together. In the middle of the quilt was a larger photo of the two of them embracing on their wedding day up at grandfather's cabin.

"This is so lovely." Sarah wiped a stray tear, and looked over at her friends. "I'm so touched by this."

She stepped forward to give each of her friends in the quilting group another hug.

Lynda Goode spoke. "Well, we're glad. And we hope you make many more memorable moments together."

"We will." Sarah smiled at her husband. As she began to fold the quilt into a square, she looked at her friend and asked. "How did you know I longed for a homemade quilt like this?"

CoraLee and the women with her smiled big at Sarah's wide-eyed look of delight.

"I know what you like, Sarah, because I've listened when you share things with me. I know what matters to you." Her friend gave her a cheeky grin.

"Thank you. You are the best of friends." Sarah blew her a kiss as they walked away.

She was just about to talk to Dakota, when Sheriff Turnbull stopped by to talk to them. "Congratulations. I'm glad to see you two are making your partnership permanent. The two of you make a good team." Hank Turnbull nodded and shook their hands.

"Thank you for coming to our wedding, Sheriff." Sarah knew he wasn't a man to show his emotions, but needed to let him know that they appreciated him.

"Of course. I could do no less for you two when you were the ones who brought the kidnapper to justice and saved that little girl's life." The Sheriff grimaced as he remembered.

Sighing heavily, he continued. "Dermot McCoy is behind bars and waiting for his hearing. He confessed to a few details. He admitted to being responsible for his wife and daughter's death years ago because he was driving drunk at the time."

Sarah bit her lip at the news. It made her angry and sad at the same time.

"McCoy also admitted to lying to the police officers who questioned him about the shooting incident near his cabin. Dermot confessed that when he first aimed his shotgun at you, he believed you were a man and not an animal like he said in his original statement. He admitted his reasons were he that he wanted to scare you away."

Dakota's jaw tightened in anger at hearing the confession.

"Finally, he confessed to making a plan to kidnap a little girl that looked like his own daughter who passed away years ago. He was trying to recreate the life he once had."

Sheriff Turnbull rubbed the back of his neck. "As far as things look right now, McCoy is in big trouble. We have a psychiatrist starting to talk with him on a regular basis already, so we'll know more in a few weeks what's going on. But, I just wanted to say thanks for all you did."

Dakota's voice. "I'm just thankful Mindy is safe and so is Sarah."

Sarah curled her hand into Dakota's arm. Fear still tried to get the better of her, whenever she remembered the kidnapping and Dermot McCoy. She was happy to hear he had been arrested. She hoped he would get the help he needed and not be able to hurt any other little girls ever again.

"My wife is full of courage. When I arrived at that mountain cabin, Sarah was focused on saving that little girl's life instead of her own." Dakota's words of praise for her, pleased her to no end.

"I'm not surprised, Mrs. Callahan." The Sheriff grinned at her. "And after all that you've been through, may I say I'm glad to see you get some happiness in life again." He touched the tip of his cowboy hat and shook Dakota's hand before he walked away.

Sarah expelled a breath. It was a relief to know that the kidnapper had been arrested.

"You okay?" Dakota whispered, as he slipped his arm around her waist, pulling her close.

She nodded. "I've just married the man I love, so I'm doing great."

"Good. I'm glad to hear it."

Dakota waved to a woman with a little girl, who walked towards them.

"Cameron, thank you for coming to our wedding." Dakota turned to Sarah and explained. "Cameron is my secretary at my office in Colorado and this is her daughter Isabel."

"Nice to meet you Cameron and you too Isabel." Sarah smiled warmly and shook both of their hands.

"We are so happy to be here with you today. You have married a good man, Sarah." Cameron spoke with a beautiful Spanish accent.

Sarah nodded. "I agree, Dakota is quite wonderful."

Cameron nodded and pulled out a wrapped present.

"This wedding gift is from Mindy and her parents. They came by the office earlier this week and asked if I would bring the gift to you."

"Oh, how lovely. I wonder what it is?" Sarah opened the gift wrapping and pulled out a Christmas card and a little doll that looked a lot like the doll Mindy had held in her arms.

"Oh my. I'll read what they wrote." Sarah's voice sounded raw as she read. *"To Sarah and Dakota. Words aren't enough to say how grateful I am to you for saving me from that bad man. Here is a new doll that matches mine. I hope you remember me always. I will always remember you both. Thank you for all you did to help me. I am forever grateful. Your friend, Mindy."*

Sarah bit back tears that wanted to fall down her cheeks as she looked up. "This gift means so much to me. Tell her I'll write her back, okay?"

Cameron nodded. "I will. We need to be going. Congratulations to you both."

As they walked away, Dakota said. "This is a very thoughtful and heartfelt gift from Mindy."

"Yes, it is."

"I was thinking of making a change in my career as a P.I." Dakota looked at her, his dark eyes somber.

"Oh?"

"Well, I thought I would hand over my current cases in Colorado to my part-time Private Investigator, Milo Stevens. That way I would be free to manage things from our home. I could take care of calls and paper work from our ranch. That way I could be at home more with you and any children that we should be blessed to have."

Sarah sighed in contentment. "That would be wonderful."

"What would be wonderful?" Annie Callahan walked up to them and hugged her son.

"Just talking about our future plans." Sarah grinned and hugged her new mother-in-law.

Annie gently kissed her cheeks. "Lovely girl, I have longed to see this day. I'm so happy that you are part of our family."

Sarah was embraced by all the other members of the Callahan family and loved being surrounded by her new family.

Grandfather walked towards them with Mrs. Moore on his arm.

"So, it looks like I have a new grandson. Welcome to the family, Dakota." It did Sarah's heart good to see her grandfather accepting and welcoming her husband.

Mrs. Moore hugged her then. "I'm happy we will all be family very soon."

"I am too." Sarah embraced this woman, who was so important to her grandfather.

Grandfather swept Sarah in a big hug. "Lassie, your grandmother would be proud of you on this day. She always wanted you to marry the man you loved and to have a life filled with happiness."

"I know she did. I think she's smiling down on us both today, grandfather." Sarah whispered and kissed his weathered cheek.

"Aye. Maybe so." Her grandfather's eyes were misty as he walked away with Mrs. Moore on his arm.

"I think my grandfather is turning soft in his old age. I

like it." Sarah beamed at Dakota who merely smiled and nodded.

Many other guests also stopped to talk to them and offer their congratulations and Sarah and Dakota thanked every one of them for coming.

After they had talked to most of the wedding guests, Sarah and Dakota walked outside the church doors and down the stairs to a small alcove by the church building.

Snow was falling softly, covering their small town in a fluffy white blanket.

"Before I forget, I have something here from our family's lawyer, Mr. McCrae." Dakota reached inside his suit jacket and pulled out an envelope.

Opening it, he took the letter and began to read. *"Thanks to your dad's will, I'm happy to give this to you today on your wedding day. You did all that your father asked of you and more. I'm sure he's as proud of you as any dad could be. Here's a cheque from your dad to get started on those dreams of yours. And congratulations on your marriage."*

Sarah gasped when Dakota showed her the cheque. "That's a lot of money."

"More than enough."

"The lawyer mentioned some dreams you've had. What did he mean?"

Dakota rubbed the back of his neck. "Well, I was thinking we could use some of it to start a foundation and build a center for missing children."

"It would help to speed up the process to help as many parents or guardians to find their missing children as soon as possible. What do you think?"

"I think that's an amazing idea. And what a great way

to help other children to find their way home." Sarah was just starting to realize what a wonderfully generous and compassionate man she married.

Dakota pulled her close. "And I have one more surprise for you."

"What's that?" Sarah looked up to see a tenderness in his eyes.

"Since your grandfather and Mrs. Moore are getting married, I thought we could build them a house on our ranch. Your grandfather loves cattle and he might want to live on the ranch to enjoy being with the animals he loves so much." Dakota waited for her response.

Her eyes opened wide in surprise and she threw her arms around his neck. "Thank you Dakota. Having my grandfather nearby means the world to me."

He chuckled and pulled her close. "I'd do anything to make you happy, my love. I'm glad you like the idea."

She kissed him soundly, before pulling away.

"Looks like I'll need to surprise you more often."

Sarah giggled and snuggled closer, resting her head on his chest.

Suddenly, the sound of church bells filled the air. The joyful pealing of bells seemed to ring out a proclamation of tidings of great joy across their small town.

"I've come to appreciate the sound of those bells." Dakota began. "My parents always told me those bells echoed the sound of Christmas, which they said was filled with hope, miracles and love."

"The two of us loving each other and finding that second chance together is a miracle I didn't believe was possible."

"I love that. Hope, miracles and love. It's definitely what we are celebrating tonight as we start our new family this Christmas Eve." Sarah's tremulous smile echoed the happiness that was in her heart.

"Agreed."

For a long time, they stood there and watched the snowflakes falling gently on the ground.

"You know, I really wrestled with your idea for us to begin a fake marriage." Dakota shifted her in his arms, and put his hands on her cheeks, tipping up her chin.

"But now I know in my heart, that choosing to have a marriage of convenience was the best thing I ever did because it brought me to you." Dakota rained down kisses on her temple, cheeks, nose and finally her lips. "I love you."

Sarah swallowed back the emotion that rose up to her throat and she kissed him back, savoring every moment.

She would never get tired of hearing her husband say the three most beautiful words in the world: *I love you.*

Excited to Read Hunter and CoraLee's Story?
Pre-Order The Wounded Cowboy's Beauty Bride.

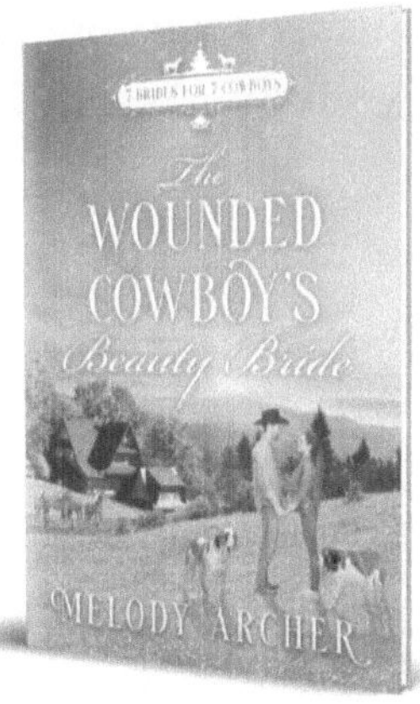

Hunter Callahan is a wounded former Navy SEAL, returning to his ranch to raise horses. He's determined to keep his distance from anybody who could hurt him... including the one woman he never stopped loving.

She's determined to break down the walls he's placed over his heart, even if it means losing her heart to him all over again.

Hunter had been badly scarred in his last tour of duty as a Navy SEAL. Returning home to his Montana ranch, he's determined to stay away from people, and focus on training Quarter Horses.

Most of the ranchers in the area and beyond know him as the horse whisperer and he runs a successful business.

His youngest brother Cole runs the people side of the

horse business for him, until something comes up and his brother needs to leave for a few weeks.

Reluctantly, Hunter manages the face of the business, until the beauty he loved years ago shows up on his ranch.

CoraLee is desperate for help. She flies back to her home town from her latest modeling assignment in Paris, in an effort to help save her younger brother from a deadly addiction to drugs and the gang that threatens his life.

CoraLee needs help, and she knows just who to ask.
The man she had loved years ago.
When Hunter finally agrees to talk with her, he insists they meet during the evening, shadows of the moonlight.

Hunter is determined to shield his heart and his face from CoraLee. The problem is… she's breaking down his carefully constructed walls around his heart.

Can he trust her to see him for who he truly is? Because Hunter thinks he's about to lose his heart.

www.memorablefictionbooks.com

ABOUT THE AUTHOR

Melody Archer lives in Alberta with her husband and their four young adults.

Recently, her oldest son married his wife from Brazil. Their family is enjoying getting to know their new daughter-in-love.

Melody loves new and classic romance movies, green smoothies and going on adventures with her family.

Melody would love to connect with you below. :)

facebook.com/memorablefictionbooks
instagram.com/memorablefictionbooks
bookbub.com/profile/melody-archer
pinterest.com/memorablefictionbooks
youtube.com/@memorablefictionbooks

ACKNOWLEDGMENTS

Thank you to all the wonderful people who helped me with this book.

To my cover designer, Wilette from Red Leaf Book Design, thank you for designing another beautiful book cover.

Thank you also, to my proofreader Cathy who patiently read through each chapter, helping me make this story so much better.

A big thanks to all my wonderful Advanced Readers (my ARC reading team), who faithfully read and left reviews of this book.

A huge thanks to my three young adult children who read through the manuscript, giving me all kinds of great suggestions on how to make this a better story.

And lastly, thank you to my husband for waiting so patiently when my writing schedule gets a little crazy. ;)

Thank you everyone. I really appreciate you!:)